MURDER AT PALM PARK

SHARON E. BUCK

SOUTHERN CHICK LIT

Copyright © 2024 by Sharon E. Buck

All rights reserved.

No portion of this book may be reproduced in any form without written permission from the publisher or author, except as permitted by U.S. copyright law.

For more information, or to book an event, contact : sharon@sharonebuck.com

To join my VIP Newsletter and to receive a **FREE** book, go to http://www.SharonEBuck.com

Cover design by Steven Novak, NovakIllustration.com

Contents

1. Chapter 1 — 1
2. Chapter 2 — 35
3. Chapter 3 — 45
4. Chapter 4 — 54
5. Chapter 5 — 72
6. Chapter 6 — 87
7. Chapter 7 — 96
8. Chapter 8 — 104
9. Chapter 9 — 125
10. Chapter 10 — 136

11.	Chapter 11	155
12.	Chapter 12	165
13.	Chapter 13	175
14.	Chapter 14	182
15.	Chapter 15	197
16.	Chapter 16	215
	More Books	223
	More Books - 2	224
17.	About the Author	225
18.	Acknowledgements	227

Chapter 1

Sarah was slumped over the table, her coffee with an obscene amount of liquid sugar in it was dripping off the edge, so was red fluid. The new barista, well, let's just say he wasn't going to be making any coffee drinks ever again.

I threw up as I was punching nine-one-one. My hand was shaking so badly that I now only had about half a cup of coffee left. I was now wearing the rest of it on my hand, arm, and the front of my shirt.

While waiting for the police to show up, it was only minutes but felt like hours, my thoughts dive-bombed my psyche.

I am a highly paid escort. I am young, cute, and deadly. I am an assassin.

No, no. That's not right. I am an opera singer. Yes, that's it. I open my mouth and beautiful, lyrical notes grace the air in the theatre.

I am a professional liar, and I am paid very well for it. What am I? I could be an actor, an attorney, in sales or advertising, a detective, or a writer.

"Seriously! Get out of your head. I can see story ideas bouncing around in your brain." Sarah had grumped at me. We've been friends since before breakfast. Actually, we've known each other since the fourth grade. We are not best friends…just good friends who know way too much about each other in certain areas of our lives. Still, when Sarah's not craving something to eat every two or three hours, she can be a lot of fun.

"What's wrong with you?" I grinned. It was just so much fun to see how much I could annoy Sarah, especially when I knew she was skating on the edge of crazy without her morning caffeine and sugar fix.

She grabbed her cup of coffee from the new barista at Coffee & Cupcakes, took a sip, put it back on the counter, and pushed it back to him. "It doesn't have enough sugar in it. I specifically asked for six shots. You didn't do that."

The guy inhaled deeply through his nose, letting the air out slowly through his nostrils, "Do you want me to put more in this cup or do you want a new one?"

Sarah snapped, "What do you think?"

"Hey, Sarah, chill." I held up three fingers to the guy. "Just put that many in the cup."

She started to say something, and I decided to shut her down. "Stop it! Tip the man."

Glaring at me, she snatched the mug that now had more sugar in it than our ancestors had had in a year, "No!"

Deciding our friendship probably needed a break, a long break, I tipped the young man. Taking my coffee and ignoring Sarah seated at one of the little tables, I started for the door.

"Hey!"

I ignored her and kept walking.

Looking back on it, I was amazed at how unobservant I was...or, just call it being too self-absorbed with Sarah's bad manners that I wasn't paying attention to the tall individual coming through the door. I was already out on the sidewalk trying to decide if I was going home to start writing a new story or if I was going to go pet the new puppies at Ronnie's pet store when I heard two double shots.

It took a moment for it to register that those were gunshots that I heard. Behind me. In the coffee shop.

Turning around, I rushed through the door. I don't know that I was thinking anything when I entered the store. My brain stops having coherent thoughts when I'm scared.

That's when I saw Sarah and called the cops.

Detective Sam Needles, really that is his name, walked over to where I was now sitting inside the store. "Please tell me you're not rehearsing a scene for a new book or something."

I shook my head. There was a small, unfortunate incident that had happened several months earlier when several mothers at the local park had observed me, Ronnie, Sarah, and Ruthie acting out a scene for a new book, thought we were trying to kill each other, and called the cops. We were but it was because I was trying to figure out the action details and how to describe it in a chapter. I'm a visual person and I needed to see a person's movement before I could write it.

Sam had been dispatched because the local patrol officers were off getting coffee and donuts or something.

Let's just say he wasn't amused when I told him those nosy mothers should have been paying more attention to their precious little progenies rather than adults on the other side of a public park who were minding their own business.

I told him what had happened.

"Was it a man or a woman coming through the door as you were going out?"

I shrugged. "I think it was probably a man because he was so much taller than I am."

Sam tried to keep from snorting. "You do realize you're only about five-three on a good day."

Huffing and trying to stand taller, there's only so much vertical height I can do even with taking deep breaths and blowing it out. "I'll have you know I'm five-four. Don't make me any shorter than I already am."

"So, the person was tall. What were they wearing? Did they have anything in their hand? Hair color or where they wearing a hat? Can you describe anything about this individual?"

Shaking my head, I said, "Um, I was kinda not paying attention. I was irritated with

Sarah's poor manners with the new guy, the new barista."

Sam nodded his head. "Did Sarah have any enemies? Anyone she was having a problem with? Owed money to?"

I suddenly realized how little of Sarah's personal life I actually knew. When we got together, all we did was talk about everyday things, nothing important, and nothing really personal.

"Sarah was dating or, rather, had gone out on a coffee date with a guy she met online. But I don't know anything about him."

I hadn't been wild about her picking men out of a lineup on a dating website and told her so. I didn't know the guy's name or anything about him. She told me I was an old fuddy-dud. Seriously? Who even uses words like that anymore? We had exchanged unpleasant words and today was the first day we had seen each other in a week.

With her being so snarky at the barista, I hadn't even cared enough to stay and ask her what was wrong. Maybe my subconscious had picked up bad vibes or maybe it was just me deciding that I'd had enough of her negativity. Whatever it was, I didn't want it in my life.

Maybe I should feel badly about my thoughts and feelings but, to be honest, I really didn't. I was sad she was dead, had been murdered, but I wasn't freaking out about it. My throwing up was more about seeing blood than anything else. I have a notoriously weak stomach when it comes to seeing body fluids, even seeing a kid spit on the ground can cause me to want to vomit. Go figure.

No expression on Sam's face. "Thought you had been friends for years. How could you not know who she was dating?"

Did I dare say we didn't have that type of relationship because that wouldn't make sense...or maybe it did. Just because we were women and friends for years didn't mean we shared all the details of our lives. Or, at least, I don't.

To share all details, intimate details, of my life involved a level of trust that I just simply do not have for most humans. Dogs, yes; humans, no.

Also, I must admit, I truly wasn't that interested in who Sarah was dating right now. Since my own dating life was minimal…who am I kidding? It's non-existent, which means, I wasn't remotely interested in who she was dating. It was different when we were both dating someone because then we had things to talk about but with me not having anyone in the romance department at the moment, I didn't care.

I wasn't sure how to respond to Sam's question, so I shrugged.

Raising his eyebrows slightly, he asked, "You do know where she lives, right?"

Snorting, I gave him the address. "Before you ask, no, I have no clue on any of her passwords or anything. I don't even remember which dating website she was on."

"Do you have a key to her apartment?"

"Um, I think there's one over the door frame." I only knew that because we had been out partying one night, I had been the designated drunk driver, and we had somehow managed to stagger walk up the four steps into her apartment building while giggling where I had to semi-lift her up to get the key.

Where was the apartment key and why didn't she have it with her? Because we had both left our purses with the bartender where he had kindly stashed them under the counter for safekeeping. The key was in her purse.

"Does she have any relatives nearby? Who is her next of kin? Do you know how to contact them?"

A red-haired woman entered the coffee shop, dabbing at her eyes with a tissue, stopped, and took a slow look around the room.

"Sam. What happened?"

"Lisa, do you have security cameras anywhere?" Sam ignored her question. I wondered if Lisa was a special kind of stupid since it was pretty obvious that two people had been killed in her business establishment.

I had known Lisa since middle school. She wasn't that bright then either; however, let me be fair and say that she did have the proverbial green thumb on growing successful businesses in our little town. The coffee shop was success number five.

Not willing to admit that, although my IQ was higher than Lisa's, her ability to connect the dots in life and become a successful business owner did cause a little bit of ugly jealousy within me.

I am a word ho, I sell my words for a living. Sometimes I'm making really good money and other times, I was eating beanie-weenies for a week while waiting on a royalty commission check. There were days where the thought tap danced its way into my mind that I'd probably make more money by selling my body on the street. I was never going to do that, but the thought did occasionally enter my brain.

Lisa pointed at a door with a plastic Employees Only sign on it. "There."

Sam walked over to the door, turned the knob, looked back at Lisa, and said, "Would you unlock the door?"

I could tell he was mentally struggling not to roll his eyes at her. The joys of living in a small town and knowing each other way too well was that we all knew each other's tells.

"Oh, yeah, yeah, sure." Lisa grappled with the door, finally holding up the key she had been trying to jam in the lock, and said, "Um, I don't think this is the right key. I'll have to go home and get the right one."

"Lisa, you mean you don't use the same key for all of your stores?" I was incredulous. It seemed perfectly logical to me that you use the same key for all your stores or, at the very least, have a key ring with all the stores' keys, color-coded of course, in your purse or car at all times.

A Bambi in the headlights look crossed her face. Shaking her head, "It never occurred to me to do that. Thanks, it's a great idea. Sam, I'll be back in a minute."

She scurried out the door. Sam and I looked at each other dumbfounded. I swear I don't know how this woman is such a money-making guru. Maybe I overthink things too much.

"What you want to bet that either the security camera doesn't work or that you can't see anything on it?"

Sam ignored me, walked behind the counter, and poured himself a coffee.

Maybe I was in shock or maybe my mind had already warped into brain fog, I don't know, but I was already mentally writing a new scene for my book because that seemed like the most logical thing for me to do.

"Harper!"

I started, looking around to see who had shouted my name.

It was Sam. He was holding out a cup of coffee. "I wanted to know how you wanted your coffee."

"Black with two shots of vanilla."

Lisa was back, frowning at us like naughty children who had been caught shoplifting expensive candy. Her stern death scare look had zero effect on either one of us. Sam had probably seen more hateful looks in his law enforcement career pulling speedsters over in our small town.

Me? It was nothing like the death stare I received from my now-deceased mother when I informed her many years ago that I was going to make my living by writing novels.

"Just because I named you Harper does not mean you need to be a writer," she sniffed. "I just liked the name – nothing more, nothing less."

Hateful looks did not intimidate me. I just used them in my next book.

Lisa's lips were tight as she walked over to the Employees Only door. On the fourth key, she finally managed to get the door open.

Entering, I glanced around and resolved to never order food from here ever again. There were open containers of cupcakes from a wholesale big box store sitting on metal shelving, crumbs were all over the floor, and open jars of frosting on what should have been a clean countertop. That was covered with used paper towels, a dirty rag of some sort, and coffee cups that appeared to have been sitting there for hours on end if not days.

Sam looked at Lisa who appeared to be oblivious to the hundred and one health code violations. "Um, you do know…"

"The camera is back here." She went through an unlocked door where there was a desk, a chair, a computer, and two camera screens. There was only enough room for one person, two if one was sitting in the metal folding chair.

Sam sat down in the chair, Lisa stood directly behind him, and I was scooched over to the side. Lisa gave Sam the password and told him how to get into the system.

We watched silently as the man entered the store, yes, it was a man, lifted his right arm and shot Sarah twice before turning to the new barista and double-tapped him. The man walked past the countertop and out through the back.

Sarah had barely glanced at the man as he came through the door. I guessed she was more intent on determining whether the new barista had put the ridiculously obscene amount of sugar in her coffee. How did I surmise this? You could see Sarah's head bent downward as the man approached.

The barista gave the man a welcoming smile as he came through the door. When he shot Sarah, the barista had taken a step backward and raised his hands in surrender. I would hazard a guess that the poor guy thought he was being robbed. Unfortunately, not.

"Do you know him?" asked Sam pointing at the man on the screen.

Lisa didn't say anything. One tear escaped from her left eye and was slowly edging its way down her cheek.

Sam half-turned in his chair. "Lisa, do you know this man?"

"Um, I don't think so."

She was lying. I knew it. I could feel it in my bones. The question was why.

"Okay, I'm going to email this to..."

"Um, I can't let you do that." Lisa was suddenly all businesslike. "I need to talk to my attorney first."

Sam stood up, looking somewhat puzzled. "Why, Lisa? I'm trying to solve a crime, a murder that was committed here in your store. There's nothing incriminating on this tape for your store."

We all backed up from that postage stamp size room.

She shook her head. "Get a search warrant and I'll be happy to give it to you."

Lisa was punching numbers in her phone, looked up, and said, "You can leave now."

Sam stood there for a moment. "Lisa, do you really want to do this the hard way?

It's starting to appear that you know the murderer and are protecting him."

She pointed at the door. "Come back when you have a search warrant."

Sam shook his head. "Crime scene. We're not leaving until we've completed what we need to do. On the security tapes, I'll get a search warrant for that."

"Are you being shaken down, Lisa?" Something didn't make sense and my brain was clicking on anything that might get her to talk.

"What part of leave do you guys not understand? If you don't exit my premises within the next thirty seconds, I'm going to have my attorney file harassment charges against the both of you."

I held up my hands in surrender and started walking toward the door. Sam had moved over to his two officers as they were collecting evidence, and they were talking in low tones.

Ideas were swirling in my head on how I could use this in a book. Somewhat oblivious, once again, I literally bumped into Ronnie as I exited Coffee & Cupcakes for the second time today.

"Oh, honey! Are you okay?" He was holding a teacup Maltese puppy. I melted looking into those sweet, innocent eyes, and her beautiful white long hair didn't hurt either. "Here, honey, hold Paige for me."

She was a bouncy little thing. She wanted to lick my face but settled for my neck when I moved my head back. My insides turned into an ooey gooey puddle of love. Little sweet dogs do that to me.

"What's going on, Harper? I heard the sirens," he paused. "Where's Sarah?"

I hugged Paige. I struggled to tell Ronnie what had happened. Instead, I asked, "Did you see anyone before you heard the sirens and saw the blue light special?"

He kind of snickered at the blue light special reference. "Those stores don't exist anymore. Nope, I was busy in the store and didn't see anything. Where's Sarah? I know you two were supposed to have coffee this morning."

Ronnie was busy looking through the plate glass windows when he yelped, "Oh, my goodness! Oh, oh, oh! Is that…is that Sarah laying on the table? Noooo!"

He put his hands to his face and started to cry. "Not Sarah, not Sarah, not Sarah."

Ronnie is definitely always in touch with his feminine side and isn't afraid to show his emotions. In all honesty, he was probably better with them than I am. He's always telling me to feel my feelings. I would except I don't know what I'm supposed to be feeling or how to do that. I don't have a good frame of reference for them. Oh, I can write about them in my books; but, in my real life, eh, not so much. This probably explains my lackluster dating life.

"Honey, I need a hug." Poor Ronnie had a cascade of tears running underneath his glasses and dripping into his beard.

"Um, will your, um, beard lights short circuit or something with your waterworks?" I was more curious than anything else.

Yes, Ronnie had his own sense of style and having brightly colored lights in his beard just added to his special uniqueness.

Hugging me tightly, I didn't hear his muffled reply because I was more concerned that he was going to squish Paige and then we'd have another death today. I could handle Sarah's untimely death but a dog dying…I'd cry buckets and buckets…for days.

I am very sensitive when it comes to animals. Humans, not so much.

Apparently, Ronnie felt Paige squirming between the two of us. "Oh, sweetheart, I am so sorry!" He was cooing to Paige and took her back from me.

"How much is she, Ronnie?" Maybe that's what I needed in my life, a cute, little four-legged dog to love.

"Harper, you can't have her."

I was indignant. "What do you mean I can't have her? I love animals."

"Honey, I know you do," he nuzzled the top of Paige's head, "but you'll forget to feed her or take her out. You're not a responsible pet owner."

Ronnie held up his hand as I started to howl in protest, "Admit it, Harper. You love animals but you'd make a lousy dog mama because you get so involved in writing that you forget about everything going on around you...including your friends."

Did this flamboyant pet store owner just shade me twice? It takes a lot to rile me up but once I am…well, let's just say it's not pretty.

"Did you just call me a witch with a 'b'?" I demanded, attempting to give him the death stare. "Also, what do you mean I don't pay attention to my friends?"

Much as I hate to admit that while he was right on the second part, I still didn't want to have a confirmation.

"Oh, please, girl. You are stressed. Go home and write it out."

That was probably a good idea; however, I didn't want to go home.

"Ronnie."

Grinning, "Yes, I'll see if I can get us two coffees to-go. I'm guessing you've been kicked out since it's a crime scene." He warned and thrust Paige at me at the same time, "You'd better be standing right here when I get back."

He bounced through the doors. I could see him talking to Lisa who kept shaking her head no. She half-turned from him, probably thinking Ronnie'd get the idea and leave. That was a bad, very bad, assumption on her part. I knew what he was going to do and started to laugh.

Ronnie scooted his bottom up on the countertop, swung his legs over, poured two cups of to-go coffee, and started to walk around the counter before Lisa even realized what he'd done.

She was furious. I could see her shouting and waving her arms at him. He blew her a kiss, I opened the door for him, and he handed me a cup.

Lisa took her outrage and aimed it directly at Sam and his crew. He ignored her.

"Here you go, sweetie. For obvious reasons, I didn't put any creamer or sugar in it." Ronnie took a sip of the steaming coffee. "Let's go back to the store and you can tell me everything you know."

Once in the store with all of the cute dogs running around in their playpen, Ronnie set up a metal folding chair next to his padded stool behind the counter. "Tell me everything."

I finished and looked at him. Emotion was starting to take hold of my little gray cells in my brain. I shook my head; I didn't like this feeling. It meant I wasn't in control, and I always like being in control. It's comfortable for me.

"Harper, it's okay, honey, you can cry if you need to." Ronnie was always good for a hug, and I leaned into him. After a few moments of feeling safe in his arms, he pulled back and kissed me on both cheeks.

"Did Tommy get coffee with you and Sarah?"

I jerked my head back. "Wha...what did you say?"

"Tommy King stopped in here before heading down to the coffee shop. I told him you were having coffee with Sarah this morning."

Standing there, I blinked my eyes several times trying to compute what Ronnie was telling me. Tommy King was back in town? I wondered why.

Ronnie was prattling on about Tommy. Most of it was not even registering until he said, "Did you know he's lost over one hundred pounds on the Go-Slo diet? I almost didn't recognize him."

My head whipped around. "Do what?"

"Harper," Ronnie sighed, "please pay attention. I said I almost didn't recognize Tommy because he'd lost so much weight."

I was afraid to ask but inquiring minds needed to know. "What was Tommy wearing?"

"All black from head to toe."

Chapter 2

I need to talk to Sam." Dashing out the store, I ran the three stores down to Coffee & Cupcakes. Sam was still in the store. Lisa had put up a hand-written sign on the door that said, "Due to unforeseen circumstances, we will be closed today. Opening tomorrow at 7 a.m."

I tapped on the door to get Sam's attention. Lisa gave me the three-finger salute. I was thinking less and less of her adult behavior, it went hand-in-hand with her low IQ.

Apparently, we were going to be playing charades. I pointed at Sam and waved my hand for him to come to me. Lisa grinned, shook her head, and gave me another three-finger salute.

I don't do well with stupid. It tends to bring out the worst in me. I tapped on her door one more time, Lisa looked at me with a snarky smile. I pulled my lipstick out of my purse, and before she could reach the glass entryway, I wrote "You Suck!"

On a very childish level, I took great delight in doing that. On an adult level, that was a complete waste of my dollar store lipstick. I'd never use it again. I was also annoyed that I had let myself be manipulated to do something that emotional.

"What do you want?!" screamed Lisa as she opened the door.

I pointed at Sam, "I need to talk to him."

"You're going to clean that off my door!" snapped Lisa. I ignored her.

Sam came striding over. "Come on, Harper, out here." He looked pointedly at Lisa, "Where we can have some privacy."

She turned the key in the lock on the door, effectively locking us both out.

Sam sighed, "What?"

I told him about Tommy King being at the pet store, dressed all in black, and how Ronnie told him that both Sarah and I would be having coffee this morning.

"What do you know about Tommy?"

Pulling up memories from high school that I'd tried hard to forget, not that high school was all that bad or that long ago, but I wasn't interested in rehashing an old life. But it had nothing to do with my existence now of throwing letters up on a blank laptop screen with fictional characters that only existed in my brain...or, maybe, it had everything to do with it. Sometimes I overthink things; okay, most things. The question becomes does it serve my everyday life in a positive way? My brain had skittered off into Never Neverland.

"Harper, do you need to go to the ER? Shock can do strange things to people." Sam's voice was gentle.

"Huh? Oh, yeah. What was your question again? I was thinking." I had done a deep dive back into those pesky high school memories.

"What do you know about Tommy King?"

I took a deep breath and let it out slowly. "Tommy was a popular kid in high school and dated a lot."

"Did he date Sarah?"

"Well, yeah. I also went out with him a couple of times." Gee, did I sound too defensive? My dates with Tommy were just to a movie and a hamburger. No sparks of teenage hormones threatening to lead either one of us down the primrose path of sin, no goodnight kiss either, no nothing.

Sam wasn't interested in my dating Tommy. "Were Tommy and Sarah a thing, an item?"

This was a little complicated. Time has an interesting way of distorting events, things people said, and how we actually remember the situations.

"They had an on-again and off-again relationship." I was careful about my choice of words. Their dating life wasn't exactly volatile, but it wasn't exactly healthy either. Teenagers are growing bundles of emotions tap dancing their way into adulthood that threaten to erupt on a minute-by-minute basis. Throw in a healthy dose of hormones from both genders and you have a mish-mosh of teenage angst that should probably stay in the blender of life until they're in their early twenties.

Sam was taking notes. "So did they date," he looked at me, "off and on through their high school years?"

I was trying to remember when Sarah first started dating Tommy. "I think they started dating at the first football game when we were sophomores."

"How serious were they?"

Shrugging, I started to say go ask Sarah, but she was not in a position to give him a verbal response. "You never knew with those two. One week they were fine, the next week they hated each other. Typical teenage dating, I guess."

"Did they date after high school? Had Sarah seen Tommy recently?"

Again, I shrugged. "As far as I know, Sarah hasn't seen or talked to Tommy in years. We've been out of school for ten years."

Sam glanced up from his notes. "Were you guys having a ten-year reunion this year?"

I had to stop and think about it. I hadn't been contacted but, then again, I'd only been back in town about six months or so. Maybe my invitation had gotten lost in the mail.

"Not that I am aware of, Sam." Trying to be coquettish, flirty, and not the uninspired writer I was at the moment, "Are you hitting me up for a date?"

Blinking his eyes rapidly for a few seconds, "No, Harper, I'm trying to find a connection to the murder."

I mumbled something, who knows what. I felt rejection once again from the male populace. I need to figure out why I make such futile inane attempts to flirt with unattainable men. I'd ask Ronnie later... maybe.

"Last question and then you can go," Sam smiled. Yes, he had a very nice smile with a cute little dimple in his right cheek. Maybe he wasn't rejecting me after all.

"Tommy's been gone for years?"

I nodded yes.

"Why do you think he was back in town?"

That was a loaded question...and one I didn't want to answer. So, I answered it the easiest way possible, "No clue."

"When was the last time you saw or spoke with Tommy?"

"Sam, thought you said that was my last question and I could leave. Now you've asked another one." I was trying not to sound panicked. "If the person who came through that door and murdered Sarah was Tommy, don't you think he would have said something to me? You know, like hello."

Answer a question with a question, it's what all the top guru negotiators said to do. I hoped it worked.

Cracking a smile, Sam answered, "You're right. I did say that. Okay, go but, don't leave town."

He smiled, I smiled. I didn't have anywhere to go.

Chapter 3

Pondering the morning's events as I drove the few minutes back to my apartment, I wondered if Tommy's suddenly being back in town really did have anything to do with Sarah.

I hadn't heard, seen, or even thought about Tommy in years. The last I heard he was working for some obscure company creating high-tech computer simulators. Sarah and I had laughed over coffee about nerdy Tommy constructing role-playing games for adults. I didn't even know what industry it was for. But this was several years ago, and I didn't have a clue as to what he was doing now.

My phone rang. I didn't recognize the number but so few people called me anymore, including telephone solicitors, I figured it had to be someone whom I had given my number to.

"Hey, it's Sam. I know you're a writer but what did Sarah do? What type of work?"

It suddenly dawned on me that I really didn't know. I knew that she had worked for several companies online but, specifically, I didn't know. Maybe Ronnie was right. I did tend to be oblivious to a number of things. Maybe I am too self-centered.

"Um," I semi-stuttered, "I'm not really sure. I know she had just recently changed jobs. She works from home, she works remotely."

I could almost see Sam rolling his eyes through the phone.

"Ronnie might know." I was trying to be helpful.

We hung up and I immediately punched Ronnie's numbers.

"Hey, sweet'ums." Ronnie was always upbeat and perky.

I quickly told him about my call with Sam. "I hate to say you're right, Ronnie…"

He giggled.

"But what new job was Sarah doing?"

"Honey, Sam's calling. I'll call you back."

Walking into my apartment, I noticed it seemed empty, lonely. I didn't have a lot of knickknacks gracing my décor. They would just be something to dust. I didn't want to think about how my interior life matched the external aspects of my apartment.

Flipping on my laptop, I decided to google Sarah. Maybe that would tell me what new job she was doing. Surprisingly, there was nothing on Sarah Gnome… anywhere. Not on Facebook, not on Instagram, not on YouTube, not on Twitter/X, and not on TikTok. The only two social media platforms I knew she frequented were Facebook and Instagram, but her pages appeared to have been deleted. They had been up just a couple of days ago because I had looked at them. This wasn't good.

Sitting there, thinking, I wondered if Tommy and Sarah were working on something together. That would be strange. Maybe that was what she wanted to tell me over coffee.

With her social media pages being deleted, it meant someone had access to her passwords or maybe even her apartment.

Probably not one of my better thoughts but I decided to go to her apartment. I felt sure Sam would go there. Maybe I'd beat him and could figure out what was going on.

Not seeing any cop cars outside her building, I went inside, found the key over the door, and let myself in. Sarah wasn't the tidiest person in the world, but she wasn't a slob either. Her apartment, on the other hand, was very messy. It didn't look ransacked per se, but it very definitely looked like someone had been through her stuff.

The sofa cushions weren't put back into place, her kitchen – the one place that was always clean – one of the cabinet doors was slightly ajar. Sarah on her worst day wouldn't have left it that way. Papers on the coffee table were askew. Her yellow legal-size pad that she always kept random notes on was not on her desk. Her laptop was gone.

I heard someone rattle the doorknob. Fear rushed through my body like a runaway freight train. For someone who normally never sweats under eighty-two degrees, I was drenched in my body fluid. I was paralyzed with fear. Standing next to Sarah's glass-top desk, I was in full view of the door as it opened.

"Sam!" I gasped, beyond happy it was someone I knew. I went over to the sofa and sat down. I was actually shaking and hoped he wouldn't see how badly scared I was.

His eyes swept the room as he entered. "Not surprised to see you here. What did you notice?"

I told him about the general messiness. "I haven't looked in her bedroom yet or the bathroom."

"You okay to walk or are you still in shock?"

I shrugged and headed to Sarah's bedroom. I wasn't going to dwell on feelings that I didn't know what to do with anyway. I could compartmentalize and think about them later...maybe.

"She always made her bed." I pointed at the pulled back, rumpled up sheets, and duvet. "Sarah never ever didn't make up her bed. Even after sleepovers as a kid, she always made up her bed before we went down to breakfast."

Sam pointed at the dresser drawers. "Doesn't like look those were opened. Here," he tossed me some latex gloves, "open them. Oh, by the way, did you touch anything in the living room?"

I shook my head. "Only the door when I came in. I'd only been here for a couple of minutes before you."

I opened the drawers, nothing looked like it had been touched. Her closet didn't look like anything had been moved around either. This was odd. The living room I could understand but why only the bed and nothing else in her bedroom?

Going into the bathroom, I blinked a couple of times. "Um, Sam, think we've got something here."

On the mirror, in red lipstick, was "You know. Why?

Chapter 4

I noticed the punctuation immediately. Since I'm a writer, that would be my natural first observation. I pointed it out to Sam.

"What do you think it means, Harper?"

That was a no-brainer question for me. Maybe I should become a detective. Better yet, maybe I should become a crime scene writer. I wondered if their books sold well.

"It's someone who's intelligent and made sure they used proper punctuation, which indicates to me they do that on a regular basis, it's a habit. They don't have to think about it.

"It also conveys a sense of betrayal, which means they knew each other. Probably fairly well based on the why question. What it also means is that whoever did this knew where Sarah lived.

"Since the door didn't appear to be jimmied when I got here, it means that someone knew the key was over the doorframe, used it, put it back, and then left. The question really is did someone do this before or after Sarah was murdered? Was she supposed to see it? Was it a warning? But what it specifically means or refers to, I don't have a clue."

Sam smiled, "Good suppositions. While it indicates the individual knew Sarah, it was not an emotional response."

I must have looked somewhat quizzically at him because he said, "If the person was angry, the lipstick would be smeared. Whoever did this took their time to write it, they weren't in a hurry. See how straight up and down the letters are? If they were upset, the letters would be slanted."

"It's almost like they were sad," I added. "Betrayal."

"Harper, you never answered my earlier question about why you thought Tommy might be back in town after years of being away."

"I said no clue, Sam." My heart started beating a little faster. This was a road I didn't want to go down. I honestly didn't think it had anything to do with Sarah's murder.

"You're lying." A flat statement from a small-town detective. Although I had lived in a large city for a number of years before returning here, I had not mastered the passive look of non-interest when someone, anyone, asked me a question.

"Why don't you ask Lisa about him? After all, they dated off and on for three years after we graduated."

"And?" Oh, great, now I was going to have to connect the dots for Sam. Well, at least a few of them.

Taking a deep breath and exhaling, I said, "Could we sit out on the sofa instead of standing here in the bathroom?"

A few minutes later, I was still trying to gather my thoughts on what to share.

"Harper," Sam prodded, "are you going to tell me or not?"

"Okay, Tommy was sorta dating Sarah while they were both in college. They were going to two different schools. Sarah found out that Lisa was also dating Tommy. He was alternating weekends with them. She just happened to come home on a weekend that he wasn't seeing her and saw him and Lisa cozying up at the movies."

I didn't want to tell him that Sarah had become completely unglued seeing Tommy's arm wrapped around Lisa and that they were smooching. That's too tame a word, they were going at it hot and heavy.

I didn't tell him that Sarah took the extra-large bucket of popcorn with extra butter that we had just gotten along with the baby bucket-size soft drink, got up from our seats, went down to the empty row behind the two lovebirds and dumped both the popcorn and drink on the two of them. She took the empty popcorn bucket and smashed it on top of Tommy's head. She also screamed some rather unkind remarks at him and Lisa.

Tommy struggled to pull the popcorn bucket off his head. Lisa tried to climb out of and over her rocking chair seat to get to Sarah who punched Lisa in the nose.

I almost dragged Sarah back up the aisle so she wouldn't be charged with assault. We went out one of the back exit doors.

As far as I knew, Sarah had not spoken to Tommy or Lisa ever again, which is what made it interesting that she wanted me to have coffee with her at one of Lisa's businesses. Maybe she didn't know Lisa owned Coffee & Cupcakes. That was unlikely since Sarah had come back a little more than three years ago.

"What else?"

"That's it."

"Did Tommy ever try to get back in touch with Sarah?" Sam was relentless but I guess that was required to be a detective.

"He tried calling her, but she wouldn't take his calls. In fact, she blocked him. He tried to see her on campus, but he wasn't allowed in her sorority house."

"What about you?"

I shrugged. "Yeah, he called me and wanted to get back with Sarah. I told him that she said she never wanted to see or hear from him ever again. That was it."

I didn't lie. She still held a bit of a grudge against him. Her version was if only he'd been honest and said he was also dating someone else, she'd been okay with that. Now, THAT was a lie. She was also dating other guys at school and hadn't told Tommy about them either. So, you had two liars dating each other. Even with my limited dating experience,

I knew that relationship was never going to work long-term.

I inwardly sighed. If only I had applied that to my own life, I probably wouldn't be divorced and living back in a small town named Palm Park with only four palm trees, hundreds of oak trees, and too many pine trees to count. Northeast Florida wasn't conducive to healthy palm tree life.

City life felt too overwhelming. At least the memories here were not as devastating as those in the city. That's what I told myself. I had to believe that.

"What did Sarah major in?" Sam ran his hand through his wavy black hair. "I'm trying to find the connection here. There's got to be one."

"Well, what about that new barista guy? Maybe someone was after him and Sarah just happened to be in the way." I probably sounded a little defensive of Sarah. I guess I just didn't want to believe someone had targeted her specifically.

"He's a nephew of Lisa's and had just graduated from college. He was working there until he found a job in Jacksonville. Chances of someone explicitly gunning for him are not high."

Sam held up his hand. "He wasn't into drugs or anything like that. He graduated from college in three years, not four. He was a nose-to-the-grindstone type of kid."

I am a persistent person if nothing else. I don't have any better sense than to keep plugging away at something until I have an answer.

"What about someone warning Lisa? If that's the case, then she'd be playing in a pretty high-stakes game." Yes, the thought had crossed my mind that maybe the murders of two people, who had nothing to do with each other except to be in the wrong place at the wrong time, were a warning to Lisa.

Sam was impassive. No sign that he had even heard me. Cops aren't supposed to acknowledge anything, I guess.

He exhaled. "Harper, why don't you answer my questions without skirting around? Seems like you have avoidance tendencies."

I hadn't thought of myself that way before. Maybe I could work it into my latest book. I'd have to google the symptoms. I vaguely wondered if they could be cured.

"It's called 'squirrel', I'm easily distracted by new thoughts." I smiled.

"Nope, it's called you're trying to avoid giving me answers that might help solve this case because you don't want to cast anyone in a bad light."

Well, there was that.

"Sarah majored in art, but it wasn't schoolteacher art. It had something to do with mechanical art." I had to search my brain. Sarah liked things that most people wouldn't call art. I didn't think mechanical drawings were art, but I am a word artist, and I would hazard a guess that most people wouldn't think of that as being a writer.

"She mentioned something about three or four weeks ago that she was working on something called geovisual art. I don't even know what that means." I dropped my shoulders and raised my hands palms up.

"Here's someone you've known your whole life and yet you seem to know so little about her, Harper. Doesn't that strike you as more than a little odd?"

Um, no, it really didn't. Was I just that obtuse about my friends? Maybe. Did this mean my brain just shut down about any human interaction that didn't involve me or what I was working on? I didn't think so but perhaps I wasn't the best judge of that. I'd have to ask Ronnie about that also… maybe.

"I hate to say it, but maybe you're right." I exhaled slowly. "I didn't understand what Sarah did and she really never talked about her work. I know that she worked for some pretty decent companies because I do remember her saying on a couple of occasions that whatever company she was working for wouldn't let her put in but so much money in her 401K. So, to me, that means she was making good money."

"If she was doing so well, why was she living in an apartment instead of owning a house?"

I laughed, "That's easy, for the both of us. It means someone else has to take care of the maintenance and you don't have to pay for it. Owning a house, you have to have someone do the lawn, pay for repairs, and you have a mortgage. Living in an apartment is a low-stress decision."

"You're not building equity in anything."

"True but it's not worth the hassle. Besides, her investments seemed to be doing well." I added, "So are mine."

"So, you knew she was working for a new company about three or four weeks ago then?"

I nodded. "But I don't know the name of it or what she was doing. I did notice last week when we were talking on the phone that she seemed a little stressed. She's the one who suggested we hook up for coffee today. Said she wanted to run a couple of things past me. I just assumed it was about that new guy she met on the dating website." I had a thought. "Maybe Ronnie knows something."

Looking around the apartment one more time, Sam said, "Okay, nothing else looks out of place to you?"

I shook my head.

"Keep the key with you. If we need to get back in, I'll let you know. Go home, Harper. Sooner or later, all of this is going to hit you like a ton of bricks and you should be somewhere where you feel comfortable and safe. If you think of anything else, here's my cell number." He wrote it down on the back of his business card and handed it to me.

Grinning, "Don't go see Ronnie. Let us do our work. In fact, I'm going to follow you back to your apartment."

Rats! I'd just call Ronnie when I got home then.

Sam did follow me back home. In fact, he followed me all the way to my door.

"Did you want to come in?" I was semi-struggling to be nice. I really just wanted him to leave.

"Yes, I want to check and make sure your apartment is okay."

That someone might want to invade my apartment had never occurred to me. I cautiously opened the door, peeking my head carefully inside. "Nope, don't see anything."

Sam walked past me, surveying the living room/ dining area, poked his head in the bedroom, and then checked out the bathroom.

I was actually a little amused. It reminded me of all the Law & Order tv shows I had watched. "Everything clear, Detective?"

He grinned. "Yes. Just making sure. And because I know you're going to call Ronnie the minute this door is shut, tell him I'm on my way."

Smiling, I nodded. Punching the numbers in as I heard the door click, it struck me as a little unusual that Ronnie didn't answer my call but maybe he was waiting on a customer. I left a message and didn't think anymore about it.

I wish I had.

Chapter 5

An unknown number popped up on my phone. Literally, that's what it said. I surmised it was probably Sam. A weird thought sprouted in my brain; I wondered if he was calling me for a date. Why would I even think that? Obviously, I rationalized, my emotions had short-circuited, and errant thoughts were running rampant through my mind. I shook my head trying to clear those peculiarities from taking hold.

"Hello."

I was right. It was Sam calling. I smiled. Except he couldn't see it. He also didn't sound happy.

"Did you actually talk to Ronnie when you called?"

Fear and a tremendous sense of foreboding washed over me. I didn't like all these emotions that kept insisting on visiting my brain today.

"Ah, no. I left a message for him. I thought he might have been with a customer." I paused, "Why?"

"Someone beat the crap out of him. He's on the way to the hospital."

I gasped. What was going on? Ronnie was the sweetest guy in the world. He would not have argued with a robber, he would give them anything they wanted as long as they didn't harm the animals in the pet store.

"Are the dogs okay?"

"What? Yeah, they're fine. The two little white ones were cuddled up next to Ronnie. It looks like he may have been trying to protect them. There's blood all over them. It's Ronnie's blood, not theirs. Does he have anyone else who looks after the store when he's not here?"

"Donnie does sometimes." I gave him the number. I was shivering. "Sam, I'm going over to Ronnie's house and…"

"Harper, you need to stay out of this. Ronnie lives over on Pinewood in the little bungalow, right?"

I nodded. Duh! Sam couldn't see that. "Uh, yeah."

"On second thought, Harper, meet me there but don't go in until I'm there."

Disconnecting the phone, I started to cry. This was not my standard wimpy cry-once-every-three-years-for-five-minutes-whether-I-needed-to-or-not routine. This was from a previously untapped deep well of emotion. I didn't know I could feel this way. I didn't even feel like this after my divorce. This hurt. It was a physical, emotional, and spiritual hurt.

I cried for Sarah and my lost friendship. I cried for the barista who was just starting his life when it was terminated so abruptly. I cried for Ronnie and prayed that he would live. I borderline wailed for the little puppies who were probably traumatized beyond belief. And, lastly, I cried for myself. That part I wasn't sure about me crying for myself except that it felt like I needed to.

Wiping the tears from my face and honking like Canadian geese flying south for the winter into a tissue, I half-expected Sam to call and ask where I was. Surprisingly, only ten minutes had passed since I had my total emotional breakdown.

Taking a handful of tissues, stuffing them in my purse for future use, I shut and locked my apartment door. For whatever reason, I reached my hand up to the doorframe and did a quick swipe. I don't know why I did that because I had never put a key up there. I wasn't prone to locking myself out of my apartment and there really was no need for anyone else to have a key.

My fingers bumped something as I swiped, and a key fell on the floor. That was weird…and scary. I picked up the key. My brain was not comprehending what I was looking at. I just stood there, blinking, nothing was registering on why a key would be over my door. I put the key in the lock, and it easily unbolted my door.

I needed to see Sam and tell him what was going on. He was sitting in his car when I got to Ronnie's.

"What's going on, Harper?" He was semi-frowning. "You look like you've seen a ghost."

Stuttering, which I'm prone to do when I'm scared and that doesn't happen very often, I explained how I had found the key over my door.

"This is so not good," I finally managed to get out. "Before you ask, I have never given anyone a key to my apartment. Not Sarah, not Ronnie, not Ruthie, not anyone."

"Where's Ruthie?"

"Oh, she's a flight attendant and only comes home about once a year. I don't know where she is at the moment."

"Her parents?" Sam asked. He had his phone out and was texting.

"Dead, have been for many years."

Sam stood there, tapping his first finger against his chin. "Harper, when you guys were acting out the scene for your book a couple of months ago, did you notice anyone…"

I started to interrupt and tell him those nosy mothers should have been keeping an eye on their kids versus watching us.

He held up his hand. "Other than the mothers at the park, did you notice anyone else? A man? Someone who didn't look like they belonged there?"

Blinking my eyes several time and exhaling through my nose, I shook my head. "I don't think so. I don't remember for sure. We were just very slowly going through the motions so I could write it down as it was happening. I really don't remember seeing anyone else there."

My brain was whirling around with the slightest of all possibilities that maybe all of this had something to do with one of my books...except I don't write murder mysteries. I write somewhat steamy romances where sometimes two guys fight over the girl.

While I had a decent following on social media, I was nowhere close to being a megastar. No stalkers that I was aware of. No one wanted to kill me that I knew of, and, if that were the case, whoever killed Sarah could have easily shot me dead in front of the store.

"Harper, stand behind me," Sam ordered as he tried the knob. The door opened easily, and he cautiously leaned in through the door.

"Hello. Police."

No answer, no rustling, no sound. It was quiet.

"Does Ronnie always leave his door unlocked?" Sam turned back to me before proceeding further into the house.

"Yes. His opinion is if anyone is going to steal anything, he'd rather them just take it instead of breaking the door or window. Plus," I sort of laughed, "he always says he doesn't have anything worth stealing."

"What about a TV or laptop?"

I looked around the living room. "He has one in the bedroom, and I don't know about a laptop. I think he has one at the store though."

Walking through the fastidiously clean living room and kitchen, I didn't see anything out of place. Noticing our yearbook on his coffee table, I did point that out to Sam.

"Was that always here?"

I shrugged. "I don't know. I rarely ever came over here. We always met at different places, like I did with Sarah."

We walked around the little house not seeing a single thing that looked like it had been disturbed from its normal place.

Sam laughed, "Did Ronnie decorate the house himself or did he have an interior designer?"

I laughed also. "Ronnie did it all himself. I don't think pet store owners make enough to hire interior designers. I know that he sometimes went to Jacksonville and designed some homes."

Holding up my hand, "No, I don't know any of their names."

"Is this a side hustle for Ronnie or did he have a degree, training, whatever it is called for interior design?"

I vaguely remembered Ronnie saying something about going to Atlanta a long time ago and taking some courses. Since I've only been back in town six months or so, I was still catching up on others' lives. I touched base with friends over the years since high school but nothing in-depth with their personal lives. It was the old standard of "Hey, how you doing? Whatcha been up to, etc." type of calls.

Honestly, I kind of thought it was rude to delve too much into others' lives. I guess that was part of my emotional disconnect with people. What I thought of as being kind and considerate they viewed as not being interested and, therefore, didn't share much about their lives. I wasn't sure how to make that connection to others. Maybe I needed to go to therapy.

Answering him, "Yes, I think he did at one time. Lisa might know."

Sam snorted, "She's lawyered up on everything. If I ask her what time of day it is she'll say, 'Talk to my lawyer.' That's a waste of time. Would Donnie know?"

"They run in the same circles. Probably."

Doing a slow turn in the middle of the living room, Sam pointed at the light fan combo. "Why does Ronnie have a camera there?"

I looked. "Maybe in case anyone does try to steal something, he has a picture of them. I don't know."

His phone buzzed and he answered it. "Yeah, okay. Keep me apprised. I'm going back to the pet store."

Turning to me, "Ronnie's on life support."

"I can't do this," I murmured, "I can't do this." I sat down, on the floor, in the middle of the living room.

"Harper, Harper." The voice sounded very far away. It felt like time had been suspended in the universe. I saw colors floating slowly around me. I could still feel myself breathing. Maybe I had died, and this is what heaven looked like. I heard someone talking but it didn't make any sense, it was only sounds, a vibration of some sort being offered up into the air. I was faintly aware that my body was being moved. I didn't know where. I didn't care. I shut my eyes and again wondered if I had died. Time ceased to exist.

Chapter 6

Opening my eyes I felt moderately refreshed. It took a moment for me to realize where I was. The emergency room. The one place I didn't want to be. I was pretty sure no one wanted to be in the hospital, especially the emergency room.

I wondered how I had gotten here. I noticed an IV stuck in my arm, that explained why I felt somewhat better than I had earlier in the day. I pushed the call button that was in my hand.

A smiling nurse came in. "Hi, there. Good to see you awake. Can you tell me your name and where you are?"

I wondered what she would do if I gave her a name out of one of my books rather than using my real name. I decided to test it out.

"Mary Savoy. I'm in Bright Springs, Florida."

She kept her smile, glancing at the computer screen. "Do you remember hitting your head?"

"No."

She left the room and Sam came in with her a minute later. He gave me a look that was probably practiced on prison inmates. A poker face that I was having a hard time reading, it was stern, passive, and not remotely amused that I had given the nurse the wrong name.

"So, you don't remember your name and you live in a fictional town?"

Maybe he'd go away if I shut my eyes. I didn't hear them leave so I kind of opened one eye in a slit to see if they were still there. They were.

"You know I can have them put you in a room overnight, don't you?" Sam sounded bored. "Do you want to play nice and go home or do you want spend the night here?"

I'd rather be anywhere but in the hospital. I took a deep breath and let it out slowly. "I'm Harper Elizabeth Rogers and I'm in the ER with Detective Sam Needles."

Sam burst out laughing. "Your initials are H.E.R., HER?"

I rolled my eyes. "What can I say? My mother had a perverted sense of humor."

The nurse laughed also. "Okay, Harper. Tell me how you're feeling now."

I semi-groaned and tried to reposition myself on the bed. "I think I'm better. What happened? Why am I in here?"

"What's the last thing you remember, Harper?" Sam asked, his face muscles had relaxed a little.

Trying hard to remember, my brows furrowed together, and my lips were in a tight line. "We were in Ronnie's house, you said something about a camera. Uh, you got a phone call and said Ronnie's on life support. That's all I remember."

"Okay, that's good." Sam did an up nod to the nurse. "How soon can she get out of here?"

The nurse left to go confer with the powers that be...at least, that's what I was assuming. I still had on my clothes from earlier, so I didn't have to worry about wearing a hospital gown on the way home with Sam.

"Are you going to tell me what happened or not?" I tried to sound demanding. This whole thing was embarrassing. I just wanted to go home and hide.

"You fainted, probably due to the shock of Sarah and the coffee guy being murdered..."

"Barista." I hate it when people don't use the right word to describe something. I'm sure I make mistakes also with the English language, but I strive not to.

Sam ignored me and continued. "Finding out that Ronnie had been beaten up and was on life support, that's when you collapsed on the floor. You went into shock, and I called for the ambulance."

"Oh, great." I semi-snorted, "This is beyond embarrassing, Sam. Just take me home and let me hide."

"You're going to be cleared shortly but I don't think you should go back to your apartment. Do you have anyone you could spend the night with?"

"Why?"

"Safety reasons."

I scrunched up my face. "Um..."

"One, I want someone to keep an eye on you for tonight in case you have any other reactions to what's happened today. Two, in case someone decides to pay a visit to your apartment. And three," he smiled, showing off the dimple in his cheek, "I don't want another murder on my hands."

Well, I couldn't argue with that logic. I didn't want anything else happening to me either. I couldn't think of anyone who would let me spend the night. They either had children, which I'm not overly fond of, or they were somewhat newly married...for the second or third time, or they weren't the type of friends who I could ask something like that.

I knew a lot of people but just not ones I felt comfortable enough asking or that I liked well enough to even spend one night at their home.

"Just take me to the Holiday Inn Express and I'll spend the night there." I grinned, "And since you've been so nice…"

Sam rolled his eyes.

"Because I know you're going to take me home so I can get some clean clothes before taking me to the hotel, I'll spring for a nice dinner somewhere if you can take an hour off to eat."

Sam had his hands in his pants pockets and rocked back on his heels, grinning. "Harper Rogers, are you asking me out on a date?"

Okay, that really wasn't the word I had in mind, but I could sort of understand where he was coming from. I guess it may have sounded like that to a guy. I was somewhat confused by my sudden burst of social niceness but then decided it wouldn't hurt to have another friend. At least, that's what I was trying to tell myself. He was cute.

I sniffed. "Call it whatever you want. I was merely trying to be nice."

He laughed. "Let's get you out of here. I'm starving."

Chapter 7

About thirty minutes later we were sitting in the local steak house and, much as I hate to admit it, it did feel like a date. We made small talk which, surprisingly, wasn't awkward. It felt like we had known each other for years. We kind of did. Sam was a couple of years behind me in school and, obviously, we had not stayed in touch throughout the years. Everything was fine until he asked the one question that made me want to lie.

"So, what brings you back to our lovely little town?" He grinned as he speared another piece of his ribeye. "I thought you were going to become the next New York Times best-selling author."

I slightly huffed. "You know, you can still make good money without being on the New York Times list. I have a friend who writes romance novels and is consistently pulling ten to twelve thousand dollars a month and I guarantee you've never heard of her."

Sam leaned back, and put his hands up in mock surrender. He was still smiling but it was a warm smile, not the kind that made you want to punch his lights out. "No offense, Harper. I thought that was the dream of every writer."

Shaking my head, "Not necessarily. It would be nice, but my goal has always been to have people enjoy my work. Plus, as Dolly Parton says, 'I ask God to give me some to share and some to spare.' I do okay, I'm not rich but I also don't have to eat beanie weenies on a regular basis."

Looking at me with very kind eyes, "If this isn't in your budget, I can pay for it, Harper. It's not a big deal."

Now, I was almost embarrassed. It made me sound poor. I thought I was putting to rest so many people's perception of writers that we were all poor, starving artists unless we had some big success like the New York Times list. I wanted to slap people who thought that writers on that list made beaucoodles of money.

Some did, but I also knew several writers who barely made their advance money from the big-name publishing houses.

Attempting to educate this one person of the public, I said, "Self-published authors can make more money than being published by a traditional mainstream publishing house.

"Also," I sniffed, okay, I'm a snob, "I can maintain control over all my work and then if I want to sell my books to a big house, I can. But," I held my finger up, "unless someone's offering something in the high six figures, I'm going to keep doing what I'm doing."

"Actually, that's very interesting." He put another piece of steak in his mouth. "I wondered how all of that works. Maybe I'll write a book one day."

I couldn't leave well enough alone. No, I had to spill my guts about being an author. "Writing's the easy part. The hard part is constantly marketing your books and getting readers to buy them."

He nodded. "So, are you going to write a book about these murders? You know, something like 'Bloodstain on Elm Street' or 'Rustic Secrets of Pinecrest'."

I couldn't help it, I started to laugh. "Those titles sound like a Freddie Kruger movie. Actually, I write fiction, not non-fiction but," I shrugged, "you never know. Of course, now that I have an in with local law enforcement. That might be a thought to pursue. It depends on how this all turns out."

Suddenly, there was a little tension in the air between the two of us. "Sorry, I,

I, I didn't mean to overstep my bounds," I stuttered. "I, I just meant…"

He smiled again, the dimples were back, he wasn't mad or, at least, I didn't think so. "No, don't worry about it, Harper. I was just thinking there's so much we don't know at this point. You saw Tommy King, our primary suspect, yet nothing's happened to you."

"Well, I didn't actually see him, remember? The guy who walked past me wasn't Tommy. Yeah, well, I'm not planning on anything happening to me either," I snapped.

"I hardly think Sarah or the coffee guy or Ronnie thought anything was going to happen to them either," Sam said drily. "Most people don't wake up thinking this is the day I'm going to die or get shot or get beaten up. There's a connection here, I just haven't found it yet."

Unexpectedly, I was bored, tired, and no longer wanted to be around people. My ability to be engaging in public and around people took a nosedive heading south. I just wanted to go to the hotel, take a shower, get in bed, and pull the covers up over my head. That was a do-able exercise.

"Sam, would you mind taking me to the hotel? I think I've had all the fun I can stand for one day."

He slid out of the booth. "No problem, let's go."

"Wait, I need to pay for the meal." I hadn't seen the waiter except to fill our iced tea glasses from several minutes ago.

"You can pay next time, Harper." Sam smiled, his eyes twinkling. "This one's on me and, before you ask, I had a free meal coming to me anyway."

He held out his hand helping me out of the booth. Maybe this was a quasi-date.

Chapter 8

Pulling around to the hotel's back entrance door, Sam hopped out of the car. "Stay here, I'll be back in a minute."

I tilted my head back against the headrest and promptly fell asleep.

A few minutes later, Sam opened the door. "Come on, sleepy head. I've gotten you a room on the second floor. It's under the name of Mary Savoy."

I grinned. "Thanks for using one of my characters but why a different name? I actually kind of like my own name."

"Because I can't have anything happen to you." He grinned, "We get rooms periodically to protect people and you're now a protected person."

Struggling to get out of the car, I smiled. "So, I'm in the witness protection program now?"

"Kind of. You're the only connection in this investigation right now. Ronnie was a year behind you in school. You, Sarah, Tommy, and Lisa were all in the same class." He scratched his head. "Honestly, there may not be an association between y'all or there may be the tiniest bit of one but until we figure out what's going on, I need to keep you safe."

Actually, it was kind of exciting to be in the witness protection program even if it was on a local level. Apparently, my sense of adventure, always on the lowest rung of the totem pole to begin with, was spiking. I knew I was going to find a way to work it into one of my books.

We got to the room door, Sam opened it for me, took a cursory look around, double-checking the bathroom to make sure no one was hiding behind the shower curtain, and said, "You've got the room for five days. If you need to or want to go somewhere, check with me first."

Walking out the door, he turned, winked, and said, "This'll give you an opportunity to work on a new book…or finish whatever you're working on. Night."

The door shut and I walked over, pushing the long u-bolt over the door safety guard. Popped in the shower and then fell exhausted in bed.

I heard a light tapping at the door, groaning, I rolled and squinted at the phone to see what time it was. It was three twenty-seven. Even in my groggy state, I knew something was wrong. If it were Sam, he would have called first. I immediately texted him.

The tapping was insistent, but it had a rhythmic beat. My heart was pounding. I was also annoyed because I had taken a shower hours ago and now I was drenched in sweat. I didn't want to take another shower.

Easing my way out of bed, I padded over to the door. I had already silenced my phone so when the light flashed indicating a new message, I wasn't alerting whoever was on the other side of the door.

"Keep them there as long as possible. On my way."

"Uh, yeah, who is it?" I tried to sound sleepy, which I no longer was. I was also standing next to the door hinges. I had read somewhere, maybe in one of my books, that if someone were going to shoot you, don't stand by the doorknob.

The voice was muffled. I tried to look out the peephole, but it was covered. That was definitely not a good sign.

"I didn't order pizza." I was trying to sound confused. The tapping continued. If the fool who was tapping on my door thought I was going to open it, they were beyond stupid.

"Hotel security. Open the door, ma'am."

"Wait. Okay? I've, I've got to put some clothes on." I really didn't want to give this guy any untoward ideas; however, I was trying to stall as long as possible so Sam could get here.

Oh, lord! This sounded like a romance novel where the damsel in distress needs the knight in shining armor riding on a white horse comes to her rescue. I think I live in my head too much. I could semi-justify my errant thoughts because of everything that had happened in the last twenty-four hours, although it felt like a week, but my brain had turned to mush, and bizarre thoughts that had never once entered my brain in my entire life were now bouncing around like an Olympic Chinese ping pong match.

The tapping suddenly stopped. I heard loud voices in the hallway and then a slam against my door. That was it! My nerves couldn't take it anymore. I ran into the bathroom thinking if someone did manage to get through the locked door, they'd have to go through the locked bathroom door. Surely, I wasn't worth that much effort…or I hoped not.

Now a different knocking on the door. My heart was still pounding. I'm not a drinker but I was thinking I definitely needed something to calm my nerves…at three something in the morning. All of this craziness was beyond out-of-the-box life for me. I was in a snow globe that was being shaken. In one sense, it was thrilling and exciting; and in the other sense, I absolutely hated it.

"Harper, Harper! It's safe. It's me, Sam. You can open the door now."

"Stand in front of the peephole," I demanded. I didn't want a masked intruder entering my room.

Standing on my tiptoes, I looked through the little hole in the door. Sam was standing back and had a guy in handcuffs turned sideways so I could see him.

I unlocked the door.

"Do you know who this is?" asked Sam. The handcuffed guy was about six feet tall and thin, but he didn't look like anyone I knew. I shook my head.

"Do I know you?" I was perplexed. He didn't answer.

"Was this the guy who walked past you into Coffee & Cupcakes?" Sam was all business.

"I, I…"

"I want an attorney." Finally, the man spoke.

All Sam had done at that point was handcuff him. All I had done was stutter and now the guy wants an attorney? This made absolutely no sense. Why would he lawyer up this quickly?

He caught Sam off-guard because he raised his eyebrows at me. "We can do that down at the station."

A uniformed officer came strolling down the hall. "Detective?"

"Take him down to the station. Disturbing the peace."

The officer did a curious side eye glance at Sam, nodded, and motioned for the man to start walking down the hallway.

Turning to me, Sam asked, "Are you sure that's not the man from the coffee shop?"

I hated to admit that I wasn't paying any attention when the guy pushed past me. "I honestly don't know, Sam." I gulped, "I really was thinking of other things." That sounded lame even to me, but it was all I could come up with.

"Was that Tommy King? Also, can we go into your room and not do this out here in the hallway?"

"Ah, yeah, of course, um, sorry."

"Well?" Sam had sat down in the desk chair. He kept his eyes on my face. I was wearing pajamas instead of my normal tee shirt; otherwise, I'd be beyond embarrassed about my lack of clothing.

I raised both eyebrows. "Well, what?"

Sam was exasperated. "You know, it's really annoying how you answer a question with a question or deflect a question altogether and change topics. Was. That. Tommy. King?"

I shook my head. "Tommy's much heavier."

"Ronnie said he had lost a lot of weight. Would that be Tommy King with the weight loss?"

I thought for a moment. "No. That guy didn't have Tommy's face. Plus, Tommy's eyes are blue. That guy had brown eyes."

Nodding his head, he tapped his chin thoughtfully. "I don't recall seeing that guy in the lobby when I checked you in. There was no one in the hallway when we came up in the elevator and no one was in this hallway when I opened the door. You're not registered under your own name."

He snapped his fingers. "Harper, did he use your name at any time before I got here?"

"No. The only thing he said a couple of times was hotel security and he wasn't very loud. He was kind of hard to hear. He had also put his hand over the peephole because I tried looking out to see who it was."

Sam knit his eyebrows together. "This just keeps getting curiouser and curiouser."

"Alice in Wonderland." I popped up with, smiling. "I know that book."

"What?"

He wasn't amused. I guessed it would hard to explain to him that playing Jeopardy on a regular basis was almost an aphrodisiac to a writer…and nerdy people. I guess I need to admit to myself that I am nerdy. I preferred to think of myself as an intellectual who can't be bothered with those pesky plebeians whose IQ is in the same realm as Lisa's. Now I am an erudite snot. What was going on with all these weird thoughts? I've obviously short-circuited my brain somewhere along the line in the past twenty-four hours. I had to admit that maybe, just maybe, that's not a bad thing.

I've been in the doldrums for several months and maybe all this activity, as horrible as it was, was what I needed to re-establish myself back in the land of the living. Poor choice of words with two people dead and one on life support. I started to chuckle.

"You do realize that none of this is funny, Harper." Sam's tone was sharp, and it was a statement, not a question.

"I'll explain it some other time to you." I took a deep breath. "What's next?"

The corners of his mouth turned downward slightly before becoming a small smile. "It's too early for breakfast here.

I'm wide awake and I have to be at work in a couple of hours. No point in me going back home and trying to sleep. You're up. We might as well go to Huddle House for breakfast."

He wiggled his eyebrows. "At least you can always come back here and take a nap."

It didn't sound like a bad idea. "Um, let me change into some jeans and a shirt." I grabbed my clothes and changed in the bathroom. Were we starting to connect on a personal level? That was scary. My last relationship, my marriage, ended in disaster. I wasn't willing to risk my emotions again. Emotions are fickle...and they lie...a lot. Push back, close off, shut down, compartmentalize, those things I could do well. After all, that's what I've been doing for months. It was comfortable. I knew deep down I was lying to myself, but I also wasn't willing to change. Not right now anyway.

I came out of the bathroom with a minimal amount of makeup on and I had run a brush through my hair so I didn't look like the wild woman of Borneo. A runway model I'm not but I'm in small town USA and who cares if I'm not a fashionista? I certainly don't and I don't really think Sam cares either. Unless you're dog ugly, I don't think most men pay much attention to a woman's makeup. I could be wrong, but I don't think so.

Chowing down on a grease-laden, cholesterol-filled breakfast, Sam mumbled something.

"Sorry, I didn't catch that," I said taking a sip of coffee.

"I said you never answered my question from dinner about why you came back here." His eyes twinkled, "Remember, I said you're good about deflecting questions and changing topics? You never answered my question."

Not wanting to pursue this unwanted topic of conversation, I went back to poking my food around on the plate. No longer hungry, I didn't want to admit failure in any part of my life. People used those debacles to remind me of how inferior I am in the universe. I realize I'm not perfect, I'm human, but I do try to keep my mistakes down to the bare bone minimum.

"Divorce." Maybe that one word would keep Sam from asking any more questions. Unfortunately, I added more to it. "I can write anywhere."

Looking up from slathering an ungodly amount of butter on his toast, he asked, "Why come back here then? I would think a large city like Jacksonville would offer far more benefits in terms of culture and artistic friends than here."

I really shouldn't have added 'I can write anywhere,' now it opened up the door for more conversation than what I wanted to explain.

My lips were set in a tight line and I just kind of nodded my head. "So, what kept you here in Palm Park? Didn't you ever have a desire to leave?"

"Nope."

Our eyes searched each other's but no magic knowing of our own inside secrets. Just two people looking at each other. No more, no less.

Pulling out his phone, he glanced down at it. "Ronnie's off life support and is breathing on his own. He's still in ICU though. Looks like he's going to make it."

He chuckled and looked at me. "Donnie's arranged for the gay brigade to have someone posted outside his room until he's better."

I grinned. "Ronnie's friends will definitely take care of him and, by the way, not all of his friends are gay."

Sam held up his hands in mock surrender. "I was not casting dispersion on anyone. It actually makes my life a lot easier to have his friends around taking care of him. We simply don't have enough people on the force to post someone outside his room and keep him safe. The ICU team is great, but they can't keep their eye on every patient a hundred percent."

We chatted a few more minutes and I could see the sun starting to push its way through the inky darkness of night and turning it into day. I loved watching the pink and soft blue rays poking their way into wakefulness. Morning was my favorite time of day.

On the way back to the hotel, Sam glanced at his phone again. "Do you know a Danny Willis?"

My stomach dropped to my feet. I gasped. The world started spinning. I felt faint.

"That…that…that was Danny Willis?"

Chapter 9

I sat in stunned silence. Even though I'm not a best-selling author, I do sell a fair number of books and make a decent living at it. I suppose at some point every writer has a stalker. I've never had a fan show up at my door before and that was more than somewhat disconcerting, especially since he showed up at the hotel. I did wonder if he was the one who had broken into my apartment or had put the key over the door. How had he gotten a key? That was the scary part.

"I take it you know him." Sam's tone was flat. "Why didn't you tell me you knew him, Harper?"

"I don't, I didn't," I stuttered. "How, how did he find me?"

"Tell me, from the beginning."

"Um, well, he started following me on social media. Then he started sending fan emails. I typically respond to people." I started to twist my hands. "He then started saying he loved me and wanted to take me out on dates. I ignored those and didn't respond."

Taking a deep breath, I continued, "I also really don't put anything really personal out on social media, so I didn't think much about it."

"What happened?"

"He started sending me photos of places where I had been, photos of me with friends, photos of me and my ex-husband…before he became my ex-husband. He'd say things like 'I could be here with you' or 'We'd have so much fun together.' Then he sent me pictures of my husband with another woman…" I paused, it was still very painful and even harder to verbalize, "in a compromising position."

"Sheet Olympics," murmured Sam.

I nodded. "I haven't heard that term before but yes. Danny said he loved me and would never do to me what my husband was doing, that he would never cheat on me."

"Did you report him?"

I just looked at Sam. The thought of 'you're a special kind of stupid' bounced around in my brain. Instead, I said, "What do you think? Yes, but you and I both know virtually nothing is going to be done. It only shows a paper trail on the off chance that I'm murdered or something. Then everyone will lament about how the system has failed once again, how the system is broken, what a nice person I was, blah, blah, blah."

Sam merely nodded his head in agreement. "Harper, how do you think he found you?"

Almost breaking down in tears, I hate all these emotions that keep springing up, I semi-wailed, "No clue. That's your job. You find out how he's done this. I'll file harassment charges against him. Send him back to wherever he lives. Make him leave me alone."

Sam looked a little awkward, which was kind of surprising considering all the strange people he encounters. Maybe he doesn't run into emotional females very often. I don't run into this side of me…ever.

"Is this the reason why you moved back to Palm Park? Danny Willis caused you to get a divorce from your husband and you figured here was better than Jacksonville?"

Well, Sam did have a way of shortening everything down to a few words.

I was defeated. I didn't want to admit to Sam that my marriage had been over for a while. I knew it but simply didn't want to acknowledge it because then it meant I'd have to take action and actually do something about my miserable existence. I wasn't actually living a good life. It was empty, lonely. My marriage was a sham after the first year. I knew it, he knew it, but we were both economic slaves. We needed to stay together because the cost of living in a decent area was high. I vaguely wondered what I ever saw in him. I was pretty sure he probably thought the same thing about me.

I was happier being back here in small town USA knowing I could always escape to the larger city if I wanted to. People here genuinely cared about each other. It wasn't all smoke and mirrors. The fake facial façade that so many wore in the city wasn't running rampant here. Oh, people would still smile and stab you in the back – it's a small town after all – but you always knew right where you stood with them. You never had to guess. Pros and cons to everything.

"Close enough, Sam." I sniffed, "Is there anything you can do about Danny Willis?"

Chuckling, he said, "Well, I can try to put the fear of God in him but, I'm guessing, since he's lawyered up, he has a fairly good idea of what we can and can't do."

Trying to remember what I had written in a book, I asked, "Can you put a tracking device on his car so we know where he is and if he's stalking me?"

"Not legally."

His phone vibrated. "Yeah, okay, yeah." Turning to look at me, "Yeah, she won't press charges if he promises to stay away from her. There's another stipulation. He's got to tell you how he knew exactly where she was. Uh huh, yeah, okay. Call me when you find out."

"Well?"

Sam dipped his head and ran his hair through his hair. "You writers."

"What?" Then it dawned on me, I laughed. "He put some type of tracker on my purse. Ha! I'd make a good detective."

"Give my guy a minute or two and…wait. That's him now. Yeah, okay. How did he get a key to her apartment? Gotcha. Okay, let him go but put the fear of God into him."

I looked at him.

"Danny said he had bumped into you several days ago in a store and stuck the tracker on the bottom of your purse. As to the key, he stuck some type of putty stick in the lock, got an impression, and had the key made. Apparently, he was going to surprise you with a candlelight dinner at some point in the near future." Sam laughed, "Romantic little devil, isn't he?"

I sputtered, horrified. "But you're letting him go!"

Sam nodded. "I seriously doubt he'll ever bother you again because we now have documentation, and he won't want that showing up in court.

"Do you remember him bumping into you?"

Stopping to think, I couldn't remember but, then again, I bump into stuff and people by accident fairly frequently and my doing that doesn't normally register with me. It was totally possible he had bumped into me, and I simply wasn't paying attention.

Sam stuck his hand out for the card key at the hotel door. I handed it to him.

"At least, you can go back to sleep, take a nap, rest, or do whatever it is you writers do while I go back to work."

"Can I go home now?"

"Danny's not the one who murdered Sarah, the coffee guy…"

"Barista."

"Whatever. And he's not the one who beat up Ronnie. You need to stay here. Do not, repeat, do not let anyone in."

I held up my hand. He ignored it. "I don't care if it's someone you've known forever and three days, text me before opening that door."

"Okay." I went into the sterile hotel room designed by some highly paid interior decorator to look personal, it failed, to contemplate life. Opening up my laptop and trying to write on my book, I just looked at the blank screen totally unmotivated to do anything. Shutting it, I murmured, "Oh, well, I tried." Then mentally slapping myself, I said out loud what the great philosopher Yoda pontificated. "Do or do not. There is no try."

I don't like him much. I took a nap.

Chapter 10

The phone started playing its annoying little song waking me up from a sound nap.

"Wha...what? Hello?" I managed to eke out. I hadn't looked at caller ID.

"Harper, we need to talk." Female voice, flat, demanding.

I was struggling to come fully awake. The voice was familiar, but I couldn't place it.

"Who is this?" I snapped. I felt absolutely no need to be polite. My phone, I could answer it however I wanted to.

"It's Lisa. Where are you? I went by your apartment, but you weren't there. We need to talk."

Bells, whistles, and fire alarms were going off in my head. Why was Lisa calling me? I didn't have anything to do with the murders.

What was even more disconcerting was that Lisa not only knew where I lived but had gone there. Obviously, to confront me about something. Why?

"Lisa, whatever you have to say, you can tell me now." I was still peeved and a wee bit on the snappish side.

Lisa sounded annoyed and was still demanding. "No, Harper, we need to meet in person."

"No."

She sounded shocked that someone would dare say 'no' to her. "What? What do you mean no? You have to meet with me."

I could almost see the small-town business mogul stamping her feet or throwing something at a wall. She wasn't used to not getting her way, she was a bully. Well, I wasn't buying what she was selling, and the buyer is always the one in control.

Grinning, although Lisa couldn't see it through the phone, I answered, "No is a complete sentence. What part of that did you not understand?"

A moment of silence, then she snarled, "Little Miss Goody Two-Shoes, always thinking you're better than the rest of us. You might be intellectually smarter than

I am, but you don't have the sense God gave a goose in real life. You'll be sorry."

I started to laugh, feeling like I had the upper hand, then realized she had disconnected the call. That was annoying and a little frustrating. It also meant she thought she was in control. That was the part I didn't like.

I texted Sam. He called a couple of minutes later. I gave him the low down and ended with, "She was threatening me. Can I do anything about that?"

Almost chuckling, he answered, "She didn't actually threaten you, Harper. She insulted you but she didn't say she was going to kill you or anything. The fact that she hung up the phone on you means she's emotional, a control freak, and not used to people telling her no.

But I am curious as to what she wanted to discuss with you. Maybe…"

"No."

"Harper, it may help us to solve the murders."

"No is a complete sentence," I snipped. "Also, when did it become we in solving the murders? You're law enforcement and I am not. This is your job, not mine."

"Meet with her."

"No."

"Yes."

"No, it looks like I'm capitulating. It makes her in control." I was being stubborn, maybe somewhat childish but if Lisa had arranged the murders of Sarah and her nephew, the no-name barista, what would she do to me?

Sam laughed. I envisioned his dimple becoming even more pronounced. "You do know that saying 'giving up' has less letters in it than capitulating, don't you?"

He was becoming annoying. "I never counted, besides, capitulating is a perfectly acceptable word," I huffed.

"Changing topics. Good news on Ronnie, he's still in ICU but he has opened his eyes."

I was silent, saying a private prayer for Ronnie and wishing a thousand stinging ants invade the crotch and cause unspeakable pain to whoever had beaten him up. Ronnie was such a gentle soul, he wouldn't have argued with anyone about anything and would have given them whatever they wanted. I was still in shock and, if I had to admit it, grief over what had been done to him.

"Harper," Sam's tone was a little softer, "you can't go see him yet. There's a very short list of who can see him. Everyone else will not be allowed in ICU."

I inhaled deeply and let it out slowly. "Can he talk yet? Tell him, tell him," I choked up, "tell him whatever he needs, I'll get it for him."

"Got it."

I sat for a moment after our call. Was I curious as to what Lisa wanted? Sorta, maybe, yes. Was I curious enough to return her call knowing that she was going to be making snarky remarks about me, my writing, my intellect? Not really, however, I was going to have to ponder on it.

A tidal wave of emotions hit me. Ambush grief it's called. Although I had thought about putting Sarah on the back burner of my life for a short time, it never once occurred to me that I might never see her again. The murder of my childhood friend, I didn't even have the words to express how devastating I felt at the moment. I puttered about the hotel room and finally made a pot of coffee. The pot was about the size of a little girl's tea party set. It had the capacity of a Styrofoam cup and a half. It would have to do and, to be honest, I didn't even really want it. It was simply something to do.

I was numb, almost like sitting in a snow globe waiting to be shaken. Shaking my head slightly, I dug deep inside myself and resolved, one way or the other, to find out who murdered Sarah and put

Ronnie in the hospital. There was no doubt in my mind that they were related in some way.

Looking at my phone, I mustered up my courage, found Lisa's number in recent calls, and punched it.

Lisa, ever the epitome of graciousness, snarked, "About time you called me back."

Trying very hard to keep my temper reigned in and not say words that only Marines and sailors use, "What is it that you want, Lisa? I don't know anything, and I don't want to waste time for either one of us."

"I'm not talking about it over the phone. Tell me where you are, and I'll come to you."

Um, no. Something was definitely off, and I didn't want her to know where I was staying.

"Lisa, I am willing to meet you anywhere in public. Just give me a time and a place."

"What's the matter? You afraid of me?" She was deliberately taunting me. She didn't realize I had been through many years of this type of emotional abuse…because that's exactly what it was. Bullying is one term, narcissism is another.

"Where do you want to meet, Lisa?" I was calm. I lowered my voice and tone slightly, letting her know she couldn't rattle my cage. I was an expert at deflecting people's questions.

"Fine," she snapped. "Meet me at Athenian Owl in thirty minutes."

I grinned. I knew George, the owner, or as he liked to call himself Adonis the Greek God. He was cute but, more importantly, I was sure he wouldn't let Lisa do anything harmful to me.

Texting Sam where I was going to be, I pulled up the Uber app and put all my info in there to be picked up.

A few minutes later, I was walking through the door of the Athenian Owl. It was a small family-owned Greek restaurant where the food was very good and the prices reasonable.

"How are you today, my dear?" George gushed as he escorted me to a booth. His delightful Greek accent, his warmth at greeting me as a friend and not as a customer, and his happiness in life always made me feel welcome.

"George," I paused, looking around, "Lisa is joining me."

A slight frown crossed his face, "I'll take care of you, not to worry."

Grinning, "Do you want me to spill some water on her?"

I laughed. He understood. "No, but it's a thought."

Lisa barreled through the restaurant door and into the restaurant. She was a woman on a mission – a frown on her face and had all the subtlety of a debutante who had been kicked off her sorority board of directors.

She slid into the booth, ignoring George. "Water with a slice of lemon and not the end of it either," she ordered, flicking her wrist as dismissal at George.

He rolled his eyes and left. I just looked at her, my poker face mask was on. This was another expression I had perfected over the years with my ex-husband. It had annoyed him to no end and, thus, provided a modicum of pleasure for me.

"We need to talk." She didn't even bother to acknowledge George's presence when he returned with her water. I, on the other hand, told him 'Thank you' for my iced tea. Good manners will win out every time.

"You know I own five businesses, right?" No preamble, no nothing. This was a woman who expected everyone to cater to her whims. I wasn't going to be one of them.

"So?" I took a sip of my tea and proceeded to look at the menu. It was merely a diversionary tactic; I knew the menu by heart, and I typically ordered the same thing every time I came here...the lamb shank exohico.

Out of the corner of my eye, I saw Mama, George's mother approaching our table. I smiled. Mama was always so sweet to everyone.

She leaned over and gave me a hug. Lisa was visibly annoyed and made absolutely no pretense at hiding it. "Eleni, what kind of barely edible food is the least likely to make me sick today?"

Whoa! Lisa had the social grace of someone looking to have the kitchen staff deliberately spit into her food.

I didn't know Mama's name was Eleni, she'd always just told me to call her Mama. All of the other patrons called her that. Obviously, Lisa wasn't going to do it.

Mama's smile never slipped nor wavered. In her heavy Greek accent, she said, "Lisa, so nice you come to have wonderful meal here."

"Humph."

I was bordering on severely disliking Lisa even more. Honestly, how hard is it to be nice to others? Well, there's always that odd moment in life where niceness flies to the moon but, generally speaking, how difficult is it to be reasonably polite to someone?

For Lisa, on a scale of one to ten with ten being easy, she was at a negative two on the niceness scale.

"Mama, you know what I like." I smiled. Mama hugged me again.

"I get waiter for you." She ambled off to another table.

"The food is despicable here."

I was ready to slap Lisa into oblivion but wanted to know what she wanted to talk to me about. Throwing caution out like discarded bath water, I semi-snapped, "You suggested this place which, by the way, is one of my favorite restaurants. Now, what was it you wanted to talk about?"

The waiter showed up before Lisa could say anything. She ordered soup.

After the waiter left, Lisa leaned back in the booth, tapping her red nails on the table. "You know I date Vinnie Piasano. Well…"

Shaking my head, "Who's that?"

Blinking her eyes rapidly, she slowly breathed out, "Of the Piasano family." Seeing my confused look, she did a slow eye roll. "Out of New York."

I shrugged.

"Oh, come on, Harper! You can't possibly be that dense…or that stupid. The Piasanos are one of the top five mafia families in this country."

"Lisa, I don't hang around criminals so, therefore, I have no clue on who's on the top ten list of whatever." I was semi-smug. Really, she was dating a mafioso guy? And, for the record, yes, I had heard of the Paisano family. Plus, I couldn't resist the little dig about her hanging around with criminals. She said I was stupid, I'm not, although I do have ambiguous moments from a lack of clarity from time to time.

If looks could kill, I'd be twenty feet underground. She continued on while glaring at me as if I were wearing a red pointy hat and holding a pitchfork with flames dancing around my feet.

"I am also dating Tommy King."

Shut the front door! Tommy could have cared less about Lisa in high school. Now, in college, that was a totally different thing. The boy had a hard time keeping his pants zipped during those teenage years and, according to Sarah when she dated him in college, he was even more randy after high school. I wondered if that continued into his adult life. Chances were the answer was yes.

"When did he come back into town?" I was surprised I hadn't heard anything about him or even seen him in town.

"He's not. He comes into Jacksonville a couple of times a month and we meet then."

"Okay, so?" I shrugged again.

A deep sigh, "For a writer, you're incredibly dense. Vinnie saw us at dinner in Jacksonville."

The puzzle pieces started to fall into place.

Chapter 11

"Vinnie was jealous? Did he kill Tommy?" I was incredulous. Would this explain why no one has been able to find Tommy? Would a guy kill just for the sake of his girlfriend having dinner with another male friend?

Lisa grinned, "He's Italian, what can I say? Vinnie's very passionate."

I snorted, "I know plenty of Italians and, yes, they can be loud and emotional but..."

"No." She paused, fiddling with her linen napkin, and looking at the tabletop. "I don't think so. I mean, I think Tommy's in Jacksonville this weekend."

I interrupted her, I was angry. "No, that's not true. You know perfectly well Tommy went to see Ronnie."

"Um, yeah, okay. I had told Tommy I wanted a Maltese puppy and I think he went to see Ronnie to get me one." She glanced up at me, slightly moving her eyes to the right.

I am a graduate of several different neurolinguistic programing courses. It was time I had a little come-to-Jesus with Lisa. I was blunt and made absolutely no effort to conceal my disgust with her. "You're lying."

"No, no. No, I'm not." That last sentence was a pathetic attempt to sound strong and confident in her words. I could see through her like I could a water glass.

"You're lying, and, honestly, Lisa, this is a complete waste of my time to even be here." I started to slide out of the booth to go home. I knew George or Mama would put my meal in a to-go box. I looked around but didn't see them at the moment.

"Wait, Harper," she sighed. "I did want the puppy, Tommy did go to see Ronnie about it but then left for whatever reason."

My eyebrows arched up.

"Okay, Tommy called me after that and said he couldn't afford Ronnie's prices. Now, Harper," she leaned forward with both hands clutching the edge of the table, "I know Tommy makes almost two hundred thousand dollars a year. HE CAN afford Ronnie's prices…easily. Apparently, I don't mean enough to him to spend money on me for a cute, little, white Maltese puppy."

I was flabbergasted. Was she nuts? I just sat there and looked at her for what seemed like an eternity but was actually only for a few seconds.

She ignored my silence. "He and Ronnie talked about their diets and how Tommy had lost over one hundred pounds on Go-Slo. Then Tommy left. I haven't seen him since then and he's not returning my calls."

I coughed, my mind a jumble of thoughts. "Um, did you tell Vinnie all of this?"

Somewhere between the time we sat down and the food arriving, I must have grown a unicorn in the middle of my forehead because Lisa was looking at me like she had never seen me before.

"Well, duh, yes, of course, I did."

"Lisa, what kind of game are you playing?" My tone was cold. I could barely believe what I was hearing. Had she had Sarah murdered over jealousy between two men and her wanting a puppy? This was sick, demented, and unbelievable.

"If you date me, then you need to know I'm not cheap." She tossed her hair and smiled. "You better pay, so you can play."

The callousness of this woman defied any logical explanation I could ever come up with. I would never even begin to think of writing something like this in a book because no one would believe me.

"Sounds like a ho." The words escaped my mouth. I guess I should care but I didn't.

"What?" Lisa's tone was icy cold, her eyes pierced mine. "What did you just say, Harper? What are you implying?"

I was seething. "I'm not implying anything, Lisa! I am flat out saying the only difference between you and a girl out on the street is your price!

"Furthermore, did you have Vinnie kill Sarah and your nephew as well as having Ronnie beaten up because you were upset with Tommy? Was Vinnie so jealous that he took his anger out on poor innocent people?"

I was shouting at this point, the other restaurant patrons were turning their heads and looking at our booth. George was hurrying across the dining room to our table.

Okay, I might not have thought of all the possible consequences of what she might do to me. She threw her water at me and proceeded to scream some rather nasty words and questioned my ancestry.

George wrapped his right arm around her right shoulder and pulled her out of the booth. "Out!" He pointed at the door. Mama came out of the kitchen with a broom in her hand.

"Lisa, you ride broom or get out before I sweep you out." Mama's tone brooked no nonsense.

Lisa, still shouting obscene words, left the restaurant. Some of the patrons were clapping.

George pulled out his handkerchief and handed it to me to wipe the water from my face. I grinned, "Thanks, George! Mama, loved how you to told her to ride the broom." Mama winked and went back to the kitchen.

He slid in where Lisa had been sitting. "My dear, do all of your fans act like this upon meeting you in person?"

We both laughed. I leaned over the booth and tapped the gray-haired man behind me. "So did you get enough information to arrest her?"

Sam slid out of his booth and in next to me while pulling off his silver-gray fox wig. He fluffed his own black hair slightly. "I had it on crooked. Good thing she wasn't paying the slightest bit of attention to me.

"But, in answer to your question, I need to run everything by the state attorney first and then see what we can do."

We high-fived each other.

"Of course, the real trick is going to be getting Vinnie to admit anything; and that's between slim and none and slim went to the Bahamas. He's got some very high-priced attorneys, so that part's doubtful. But we basically have Lisa knowing or even instigating a murder-for-hire situation and that we can do something about."

"Hopefully, that witch will roll on Vinnie to save her own skin." I added smirking.

"We'll see. Now, George, what do you have for dessert?"

George bounced up like a Jack Russell terrier. "I think we still have some baklava cheesecake."

Chapter 12

As predicted, Lisa tried to roll on Vinnie. Also, as predicted, Vinnie disavowed any knowledge of the murder of Sarah and Lisa's nephew. In fact, he said he had met Lisa on a dating website, but they had only gone out a couple of times.

He had been adamant, through his attorneys of course, that they weren't dating, and he barely knew who she was.

Ronnie was still in ICU but was, hopefully, going to be moved into a regular room within the next couple of days. He was allowed to have visitors if and only if his gay brigade knew the person; otherwise, they wouldn't let anyone in to see Ronnie. I was allowed to see him.

He was still hooked up to all sorts of tubing that made little gurgling sounds from time to time, but his smile outweighed anything he was going through.

"Oh, honey, how are you?"

I leaned over and gave him a hug. He couldn't hug back but I heard a sniffle and that was good enough for me.

We chatted about nothing for a couple of minutes before I asked him, "Any clues?"

"No, as I told the cops, Detective Sam, I don't really remember anything. I was playing with the puppies in their little playpen when the door opened. It was a guy dressed all in black and when I stood up, he punched me in the face, and I fell down on the floor."

Ronnie's eyes welled up with tears. "Harper, he just kept punching me over and over. Then he started kicking me, I screamed but, you know, no one can hear anything in another store, it's too far away. I told him to take the cash in the register, but he kept saying, 'Where is he? Where is he?' I have no clue who he's talking about, Harper. I told him to take the money, but he just kept wailing away on me."

Ronnie's tears were rapidly exiting his eyes and running down his cheeks. He sniffled, "Honestly, Harper, he could have had anything in the store. I wasn't going to fight him."

Tears were now pouring down his face. "Honey, I like to think I'm brave but I'm a big old wimp. I covered up my head and curled up in the fetal position, trying to protect the puppies. I must have passed out. I don't remember anything other than that."

I swallowed, hard. I patted his hand. Then I started to cry. What is up with all of these emotions I keep having?!

Ronnie tried to wipe the tears from his eyes, but he had so many IV lines in him that he couldn't do it. Donnie must have suspected something was up or he was listening outside the door because he came into the room, glanced at me, and then proceeded to press a tissue against Ronnie's eyes.

"Harper, honey, I think Ronnie's tired." He was being so gentle. I nodded.

"Harper, it's okay to let your emotions out," Ronnie whispered as he tried to smile between the tears. "You've been wrapped up too tight for far too long."

Rats! Tears were now cascading down my cheeks. I didn't like these feelings, but Ronnie was probably right. I had been hiding from these emotions for far too long. Maybe it was time to feel the feelings. Inwardly, I smiled because I hated that term. It reminds me of stoned hippies from a bygone period of time.

"One last thing, Harper."

I turned to look at him while blowing my nose.

"It wasn't Tommy who did this to me. I do know that much."

Nodding and zombie-like, I left Ronnie's room. I was halfway down the hallway when Donnie ran up and tapped me on the shoulder.

"Harper…"

"I'm sorry. I didn't mean to upset him." I sniffled.

"No, no, that's not it." Donnie looked around to see if anyone was near by or even paying attention to us. There wasn't. "I have the security camera tape."

I whipped my head around to look him full in the face. "I didn't know Ronnie had a security system in the store."

"No one did," he whispered. "I had just set it up a couple of days before he got beat up."

"Donnie, did you recognize the guy who beat up Ronnie?" I held my breath.

He grabbed my hand. "Oh, honey, it was so hard to watch. I threw up." He paused, "I've never seen that guy before. But here's the thing, Harper, the only other male who'd been in the store that day was Tommy. Do you think that's what the attacker meant when he kept saying, 'Where is he? Where is he?' I mean, that's the only thing I can think of."

Could it possibly be two different people, and these were actually two separate incidents? Unlikely in my mind. Maybe this whole thing had nothing to do with Vinnie but everything to do with

Tommy and Lisa. What was the connection?

"Donnie, did Ronnie tell you what he and Tommy talked about?"

Donnie lifted his shoulders and let them drop. "He said they talked about that Go-Slo diet, and that Tommy had been seeing Sarah but that they wanted to take their time and see if things might work out again for them."

"Was he seeing her in Jacksonville?"

"Yes, they'd gone out a couple of times. Apparently, they were on some dating website and re-discovered each other." He kind of giggled. "Not like he couldn't have picked up the phone and called but whatever."

I smiled. Sarah would have let him make the first move on doing that. Interesting that they connected on a dating website. I wondered if this was what Sarah wanted to talk to me about...dating Tommy again. I'd never know. Maybe I wasn't being a good enough friend to Sarah by becoming annoyed at her and not staying long enough to listen to whatever she had to say. I did feel sadness and remorse.

"Apparently, they ran into Lisa at one of the restaurants. Tommy told Ronnie he met Lisa on the same dating site that he did Sarah, and they went out a few times, but he decided she was too possessive and didn't want to date her anymore. He asked Ronnie how he could get rid of her because she was blowing up his phone with text messages."

Everything suddenly jumped into high gear for me.

Chapter 13

Sitting across the table from Sam, I was excitedly telling him what I thought had happened.

He scratched his head and lifted his coffee to his lips. Pausing for a moment, "That's a possibility, a little convoluted but a possibility."

"Don't you see how Lisa has manipulated all of this?"

"Harper, you're forgetting an important thing here. Why would Lisa have her nephew killed? That makes no sense."

I shook my head. "Maybe it was an accident…"

"No, that was a deliberate murder. The perpetrator shot Sarah, walked over, and shot her nephew. There wasn't a pause, a slowing down, nothing. It was intentional."

"What about Lisa's sister Ellenore? Is she blaming Lisa for her son being murdered?"

Sam held up his hand. "Harper, I can only tell you so much. This is an ongoing investigation. Did you know Ellenore in school?"

"No. She was several years younger than me. I don't really remember her from school."

"Only thing I'm going to say is that they aren't, um, close." Flashing his dimple at me, yes, he smiled. "So does our having coffee again mean that we're dating?"

My cup was halfway to my mouth and I'm sure I looked like Bambi in the headlights. I was flustered and sputtered, "Wha…what? Um, no, I…I don't know. Are we?"

The caffeine in the coffee must have unleashed ping pong balls in my head because I couldn't put two coherent sentences together and sound reasonably intelligent.

Sam laughed. "Stop sweating, Harper. I'm not asking you to marry me. Coffee dates are just two people getting together, nothing more, nothing less. Don't read anything into this. I'm just messing with you."

Okay, this cop finally had a sense of humor. I guess that's a relief. My hand was still shaking as I took a sip of the now lukewarm coffee. Apparently, the adrenaline rush caused my hands to absorb all of the heat from the cup.

"Okay, since that threw you for a loop," Sam was still laughing, "let's go back for one last thing. Vinnie Piasano is an innocent bystander in all of this."

I nodded. I had already figured that out. This was all on Lisa. That conniving, evil woman. Who did she date in high school? I couldn't remember. Why? Probably because I didn't care and, more than likely, I was wrapped up in my own intellectual snobbism. Maybe she didn't even date in high school. A lot of us didn't.

Looking up a number in my phone, I discovered I did have it. I was surprised. It was from so long ago I wasn't even sure if it was still in existence. I punched it.

"Yes?" The voice was wary, flat, and while not particularly friendly, at least it wasn't hostile.

Summoning up my courage. I asked, "Did you date Lisa in high school?"

"No."

"Do you know if she did and, if so, who did date her?"

"Don't know."

This was equivalent to pulling embedded teeth. "Do you know anyone who might know?"

"No."

"Do you want to meet? To talk about all of this?"

"No."

I felt defeated. No point in pursuing this any further. I started to hang up.

"Maybe." The tone had softened slightly.

Cautiously ecstatic, I asked, "What if we happened to bump into each other at BDubs around three in Jax?"

"I don't want company."

"Totally understand and I don't either. If that happens, go to our backup place."

The phone disconnected. I semi-chuckled. Unless Lisa had my phone bugged, unlikely since I kept it with me at all times, or maybe had bugged my car. I didn't think she'd do that, but I didn't know for sure, and I specifically didn't know if she even knew how to do that.

I called for a rental car, and they said they would pick me up. It was going to be cutting it tight to make the three p.m. time but I was determined to do it.

Walking into BDubs, I looked around for a booth, spotting my person, I walked over and slid into the red-vinyl booth.

I smiled, "It's been a long time, Tommy."

Chapter 14

He smiled back. The tension on his face was evident but he didn't look like he had aged since high school.

"Harper, good to see you."

"You really have lost some weight."

He grinned, looking down at his beer. "Well, I put on twenty pounds in college. You know, the old freshman year weight gain thing. I just kept on pounding the beer and eating fast food like crazy after college and the next thing I knew I was seriously fat. Plus, I felt like crap all the time. Not to mention, I couldn't get any dates."

Mr. Romeo not getting girls? That was a revelation, and, not to mention, was probably a devastating blow to Tommy's ego.

He had thoughtfully ordered me a beer and I took a sip. I hadn't had a beer in years and thought back to the last time Tommy, Sarah, and I had been at a bonfire and drank a couple. That was a fun memory.

"Anyway, I decided I needed to," he looked up, "wanted to change things in my life. I'm not getting any younger…"

"We're not that old," I interrupted him.

"True, but I was thinking I wanted to get married, have a couple of kids, and be part of the American dream."

Really? I never thought Tommy would ever have any desire for that. I always figured he would be a playboy until the day he died.

"Anyway, so I took part in the Go-Slo diet program, worked out in the gym…"

"Yes, I noticed your muscles," I said admiringly.

He blushed slightly. "And started dropping weight like crazy. No pills, no steroids, no nothing. Just cutting gluten and sugar out of my diet, eating a lot of fresh fruits and vegetables, and then giving myself one cheat day a week. This beer," pointing at it, "is on my cheat day for this week. I can have two, no more."

"So, how did you and Sarah hook up again?" I prompted him.

He named the website. Yes, I knew the one. Sarah had dated a couple of men from it and was always telling me this was the way to get back into the dating scene after my divorce. I had been reluctant at best to do it. Maybe I should have.

"You know," he looked at me shyly, "I never did stop loving Sarah."

I started to interrupt but he raised his hand. "We were both young, foolish, teenage hormones and emotions running rampant. Neither one of us was ready to settle down. But now," he opened his hands and waved them outward," we were both at a different point in our lives. We talked quite a bit on the phone before deciding to meet in person.

"Harper, I was straight up and told Sarah I was dating several women, one who was Lisa, and she said she was dating several men as well. We had run into Lisa at a restaurant, and she invited us to have coffee at her shop in town. I haven't been in town much since we left school, and it sounded like a good idea. Of course, I knew the gossip would start the minute anyone saw me and Sarah together.

"Honestly, Harper, we were just going to meet to have coffee and talk. We were still in the catching up phase and getting to know each other as adults."

"Was Lisa okay with you dating Sarah?" I almost whispered.

Tommy frowned and rolled his eyes. "I did tell every woman that I was seeing that I was dating other women. I was being honest and upfront with that.

"Initially, Lisa seemed to be okay with that. We only went out two or three times. And, before you ask, no, I did not sleep with her. We only went out to eat in Jacksonville."

"Donnie told me that you had talked with Ronnie that she was being too possessive. What happened?"

He shook his head and shrugged. "I really didn't understand why she got upset when I said I thought it was best for us to part as friends and date other people.

"Honestly, Harper, there just wasn't any chemistry and I didn't want to waste my time. Also," he sighed, "she isn't the easiest person in the world to talk to, and I hated the way she was so dismissive to waiters."

"She's rude." I jumped in there.

"Yes. Anyway, I did call her and let her know we should go our separate ways in terms of dating. I didn't text her." He laughed.

"You have grown up," I giggled.

Nodding, "Told you. Anyway, she seemed to be okay with that and then about a week or so ago she started blowing up my phone with messages saying she missed me, that she thought we had something special together, blah, blah, blah. Then she said she wanted a Maltese puppy."

I raised my eyebrows.

"Yeah, I was thinking what does a puppy have to do about anything? Anyway, she invited me and Sarah to have coffee in her shop. I thought that meant she was being nice. So I told her yes, Sarah and I were going to have coffee at her place. That was it."

"Tell me about the puppies. She said you were going to buy her one."

Shocked. "Really? No, I was way early for meeting Sarah and decided to stop in and see Ronnie for a few minutes. I love puppies and all animals in general, but I never had any intention of purchasing an animal for Lisa." He semi-laughed, "I thought she'd make a rotten pet mom. Ronnie thought the same thing. No, I wasn't going to buy an animal for her."

"Did you tell her that?" I was curious. More bells and whistles were going off in my head.

"Yeah, sure I did, but she said if I'd buy her a puppy, she'd leave me alone. Essentially, Harper, that's blackmail and once that starts, it never ends. I wasn't going to do that."

Oh, Lisa, Lisa, liar, liar, pants on fire.

A thought occurred to me. "Do you know if Lisa was ever married?"

"Um, I don't think so. Based on what she was telling me, she just, ah, dated a lot. If I had wanted to, it would have been easy to sleep with her. I just didn't want to go that route. Something kept stopping me." He grinned and winked, "See, I have grown up."

Raising my barely touched beer, "Indeed, sir, you have. I'm proud of you."

"I just can't figure out why anyone would want to kill Sarah." Tommy was genuinely sad. His eyes watered for a moment.

"Tommy," I didn't know how to ask this but proceeded anyway, "why was Sarah so grumpy and anxious? You already know I was going to have coffee with her. She seemed really out of sorts, almost mad."

Blowing air through his nostrils, "She had texted me early that morning and said Lisa had messaged her saying to leave her boyfriend alone because she wasn't going to have another woman stepping into her place. Sarah wanted to meet somewhere else for coffee, but I said Lisa told me she never came into

Coffee & Cupcakes, and I didn't think it was that big a deal to keep our appointment.

"I feel so guilty about this, Harper," Tommy's voice broke. "What if we had gone somewhere else? Sarah would still be alive."

"Do you think Lisa had anything to do with this?" I was cautious because I was trending on thin ice with this question.

Tommy shook his head. "She's possessive, just like she was in college, but I can't imagine she'd do something like that. Plus, she would have had to hire someone to do it."

"Why do you keep looking at the door?" I had noticed over the course of our conversation that his eyes kept flickering to the door every time it opened.

"I just want to make sure Lisa doesn't barrel in here. I don't want a scene."

Something wasn't right. I started to feel a slight prickle at the back of my head. There were starting to be some inconsistencies.

"Okay." I needed to go back to the hotel and make some notes on paper. I needed to see everything written down. There was something obvious I was missing.

"Tommy, I know this is so hard." I was trying to be sympathetic. I did think he was sad about Sarah's death but was it for the same reason that I was? I wasn't sure.

He nodded with a sad expression.

"Changing topics," I said brightly, "what are you doing these days? What kind of job do you have? I'm writing, a book author, as you probably know from Sarah. I have ten books out now."

"Hey, that's terrific. On me, just kind of boring stuff. I'm a computer video programmer."

"That sounds interesting."

He laughed. "You don't have to humor me, Parker. You're into words and I'm into coding with a lot of strange symbols and numbers."

I snickered. "Okay, you got me, Tommy. I was trying to pretend to be interested in that. But you're right, I don't understand it and I don't care. Listen, I need to go. I'm on deadline with a new publisher and I need to get something out to her before she wants her advance money back."

Tommy's eyes narrowed. "Thought you were an independent publisher."

He'd done his research on me.

"That's true under my real name. I am also a ghostwriter for a small publishing house, and she wants the two chapters I've been working on." I lifted my hands up. "Hey, a girl's gotta do what a girl's gotta do to make money in the writing biz."

As I slid out of the booth, he asked, "What's the topic?"

"Mortgages, it's for a guy out of Chicago."

He nodded. "Take care, Harper."

As I walked out of the restaurant, I could feel Tommy's eyes boring a hole in me. I almost sensed he didn't think I believed him on everything.

I didn't.

Chapter 15

Tried calling Sam on the way back to Palm Park, but it kept rolling into voicemail. Finally, I decided to leave a message.

I also did a voice to text message, and it was a good thing I looked at it before I hit send. It had a lot of incorrect words. I tried correcting them as I was driving but it wasn't working out well and caused me to spew a lot of naughty language. I finally just deleted the text message. He either would or wouldn't call me from my voicemail message.

Everything was swirling around in my head. Occam's Razor theory kept bouncing around in my head. The simplest answer is usually the right one. Maybe I was overthinking everything. As a writer, I tend to do that because I live in my head. Thoughts are the horses on the merry go-round. They go up and down while going endlessly in a circle.

I was almost back to the car rental place when Sam returned my call.

"Yes?" I heard a smile in his voice. "Are you wanting to go for coffee again?"

I couldn't help it, I laughed. "What about dinner instead? I've got tons of info, stuff, to run by you."

"Do you want to do steak again or do you want seafood?"

"Wherever we go, I want anyone spying on me, us, to know we're out in public but," I paused, "we need to be in a booth so I can spread out some papers for you to look at."

"Steak. Can you be there in twenty or thirty minutes?" I could hear him smirking. "I'm guessing I need to bring paper and a couple of pens. Am I right?"

"B-I-N-G-O, B-I-N-G-O, B-I-N-G-O, and bingo was his name-o." I singsonged.

"Have you been drinking?"

Giggling, "Two sips of beer does not constitute drinking, so the answer is no. See you in a few minutes."

I had the car rental place drop me off at the steak house. At some point, I was going to need to pick up my car from

Ronnie's. As I entered, the hostess had her pasted fake smile on with the menus in her hand, turned, and waved for me to follow her.

Sam was already seated and had placed sheets of paper with several different pens on the table.

The server brought us iced tea and left.

"Sam, I think this whole thing with Sarah, Ronnie, Lisa, Lisa's nephew, Tommy, and the unknown killer is like a soap opera." I wrote each person's name on a separate piece of paper. "By the way, while we're sitting here, can you run a check on Tommy King and see what he does for a living, what company he works for, anything you can find on him?"

He looked at me for a moment, slid out of the booth, held his finger up, and walked out the door with his phone pressed to his ear.

I jotted down everything I could think of on each person.

Sam came back in, ignoring people looking at him, and said, "Done. Should have something within a couple of minutes. Meanwhile, back at the farm, what do you have?"

"Before we start, do you have any new suspects or more info?" I looked at him hopefully.

A slight shake of his head. He tapped his finger on one of the papers.

"Okay, here goes." I pointed at Sarah's paper. "Sarah dated Tommy in high school and off and on in college. They hooked back up through a dating website. Tommy allegedly made the first move on contacting Sarah, that I do believe. Sarah had used this website before but," and I held up my finger, "she never told me anything about who she was dating."

"I still can't believe you were friends since the fourth grade and you knew so little about her personal life," Sam mused.

Snapping at him, "I've told you before, that implies a level of trust I'm not comfortable with. Sarah and I had gotten into an argument last week about her using dating websites to find men. She told me she knew this guy and he was okay. She had dated him before and…" I let my voice trail off. I was thinking.

Somewhat shaking the cobwebs from my head, I continued, "She called me an old fuddy-dud. Us having coffee was the first time in a week we had talked or seen each other. Truly, Sam, I just wasn't interested in who she was dating."

Feeling what I thought was an irrational display of emotions, I immediately tried to compartmentalize it. What was this sensitivity I had? Guilt, remorse, anger? Maybe all of that and more. I just couldn't process it at this moment.

"Do you think it was Tommy she was referring to?" Sam asked.

"Um, maybe, probably but that doesn't explain why she was so grumpy. If she were dating Tommy and was happy about it, she'd be bouncing around. She was just flat out being witchy." I paused.

"Having coffee at Coffee & Cupcakes was a normal thing for us. It's not like it was out of the clear blue sky."

I snapped my fingers. "Wait! Tommy lied."

Sam took a sip of his tea. "How?"

"Tommy said Lisa told him that Sarah never came into the shop. That's a blatant lie! We usually had coffee there at least every other week and usually once a week."

I was getting worked up. "I don't think Tommy even asked Ronnie about purchasing a puppy. He's lied the entire time.

"Sam, Tommy's the one who planned this whole thing, not Lisa!"

His phone pinged. He looked at me. "Yeah. Really. Okay. Thanks."

"What?" I was past curious. I was drumming my fingers on the tabletop.

"Tommy is a computer video programmer, works for a legit company in the Atlanta area, and is on vacation." Sam tapped his iced tea glass. "Harper, you're bouncing all over God's green acres on this. Let the police handle it. We do this every day, you don't."

I was rebuffed. We ate dinner in silence. It reminded me of so many times with my ex-husband when we went out to eat. I didn't like this feeling.

"Sam?"

Looking up from his last bite of steak, "Yeah?"

"Let me just run all of this through to see if it helps on anything."

He just nodded.

"Tommy found Sarah on the same dating website as Lisa. He was dating both of them at the same time. Lisa was possessive, according to Tommy, and Ronnie confirmed that. Vinnie didn't have anything to do with anything except for going out with Lisa a couple of times. With me so far?"

He nodded.

"What if Lisa was insanely jealous and didn't want Tommy dating Sarah anymore? And what if Tommy was going to dump Sarah and continue to date Lisa but Lisa didn't know he was planning on dumping Sarah? What if Lisa was so jealous about their relationship, a relationship that went back years, that she didn't think she stood a chance against Sarah unless Sarah was out of the picture?" I paused for air.

"That's a lot of ifs," said Sam drily, pushing back his plate. "You up for splitting a dessert?"

I nodded. I could let real food go but I was always ready for dessert. I was convinced there were two separate compartments in my stomach – one for food and the other for dessert. I could always find room for dessert regardless of how much other food I had eaten.

He flagged our server and ordered crème brûlée. I might could, maybe, fall in love with this man. Oh, no, no, no! What was happening to my brain and my emotions? It was the dessert thing,

I kept saying over and over in my head. Shaking my head, hopefully eradicating those errant thoughts on consuming an ungodly amount of decadent sugar, I focused back on the murders.

"Harper, how do you explain the murder of Lisa's nephew? Also, what about the guy who beat Ronnie up and kept saying, 'Where is he? Where is he?', who or what is that referring to?"

Breaking the sugar shell on the crème brûlée, I didn't give Sam a chance to do it first. In my defense, he was a wee bit on the slow side, and I decided someone needed to break it first and it might as well be me. I spooned a mouthful of the delightfully sinful vanilla custard and allowed it to slowly melt in my mouth before I responded.

"Since I think Lisa is cra-cra…"

"There's no proof of that, Harper. That's called slander."

"Yeah, whatever, it's just us talking," I waved my spoon at him making sure there was nothing on it. I didn't want any of the ooey-gooey goodness going anywhere except in my mouth. "What if she thought Tommy was not going to leave Sarah for her and she hired a hit man to kill them both? Maybe the guy thought her nephew was Tommy and when he realized he had accidently killed the wrong man, he went after Ronnie thinking Ronnie could tell him where Tommy was."

Sam had taken his knife and sliced the crème brûlée in half. "Your side, my side. You can't eat what's on my side."

"Spoil sport." I grinned, happily digging into my side even more.

"So, this whole thing really just comes down to jealousy. That's what you're saying." He wasn't eating his side as fast as I was enjoying mine. "If Lisa couldn't have Tommy, no one could. Is that it?"

I nodded. "I'm guessing Lisa must have told him or texted him something to that effect and that's the reason why he kept looking at the door at BDubs. He thought she was going to kill him."

Sam just sat, looking at me and tapping his spoon on the side of the dessert plate. His brows were slightly knit together, he was thinking.

The sugar was causing my brain to go into overdrive, and I couldn't keep my mouth shut. "You know, it's not that hard to find someone to murder someone. You can find all sorts of unsavory characters on the dark web."

Sam semi-rolled his eyes at me. "Really? Unsavory characters and the dark web in the same sentence? Isn't that redundant, Harper?"

Well, yeah, it was. I could blame it on the sugar or the fact that I liked to do research for my books, and I just happened, it was an accident I swear, I found a website on the dark web where, theoretically, you could hire someone to murder anyone you chose. Coward that I am, I decided I didn't need to do any more research. That was the one and only time I went to the dark web. It's too scary for me.

"Yes, it is, however, you got to admit, there's a strong possibility I'm right."

"Maybe," he was non-committal. "You going back to the hotel or do you want me to take you home?"

Since I didn't have any weapons of mass destruction at home for protection and I wasn't overly excited that Lisa may want to visit me at an odd hour of the night, I opted for the hotel.

As we were driving to the hotel, I asked, "Can you subpoena Lisa's phone and computer records?"

Sam did a side eye glance, sighed, and said, "Harper, there's more to police work than having an idea and then trying to make it work or fit with preconceived ideas."

He smiled, "You've come up with some good ideas though. Maybe you can incorporate them in your next book."

A flash of inspiration came to me. "I'm right and you know it, Mr. Detective." I laughed.

He didn't say anything for a moment, then, "You could also be wrong."

I didn't say anything because, yes, I could be wrong, but I didn't think so.

Pulling up to the hotel, Sam unlocked the car doors, smiled, and nodded. "Don't let anyone in unless it's me."

No one was in the elevator area or in the hallway, I checked everywhere in the room where someone could hide. I was alone.

Blame it on the sugar rush but I had an idea to start a new book. When I'm in the zone, I am absolutely oblivious to the time. Stretching, I thought I had only been writing for an hour. It was more like six hours. No wonder I was tired.

Making sure the door was safely secured, I turned in for the night. I had just gone to sleep when the fire alarms started going off. I was so groggy, that the piercing sound of the alarms barely penetrated the reptilian part of my brain, I rolled over and went back to sleep.

Chapter 16

Around ten a.m. my phone started its annoying little happy music alerting me that someone was up and needed my attention.

"Yeah." I was barely coherent.

"Harper, I wanted you to be the first to know that Lisa has been arrested and charged with the murder of her nephew and Sarah."

Sitting up quickly caused the blood flow to my brain to drop sharply. I could feel my eyeballs trying to focus.

"Sam? Really? How? What?"

A soft chuckle, "Were you sleeping?"

"Yes, I didn't go to bed until somewhere around four, I was writing on my book." I was trying to wipe the sleep out of my eyes. "Details, Sam, give me details."

"Lisa went by your apartment last night, you weren't home, and she decided you had to be in a hotel somewhere.

"Apparently, she thought if she started a fire in the hotel, you'd have to run down the stairs, and she could talk to you."

"About what?" Lisa was sounding more and more unstable to me.

"She's convinced that you were trying to take Tommy away from her. First, Sarah, and then you."

"You're kidding!" I was flabbergasted. "I wouldn't have Tommy for a million dollars."

Sam chuckled. "Anyway, when you didn't come down the stairs, she had a total mental breakdown in the stairwell. Security called us and we arrested her for destruction of hotel property. And that's when it became very interesting." He stopped talking.

"Seriously, Sam, you just stop and don't say anything else." I tried to sound annoyed, but I was actually kind of laughing because it sounded funny. Honestly, if I wrote this in a book, no one would ever believe me. The crazier something sounds, the more likely it is to be true.

"What did she want to talk to me about?"

"Said she wanted to let you know that Tommy was in love with her, and you should stop seeing him."

"Seriously, Sam, I've only seen him less than a handful of times since college. Yesterday was the first time in years I've seen him. Wait! How did she know I'd seen him?"

"He called and told her. Anyway, she suddenly spouted out that she was going to do to you what she'd done to Sarah. At that point, we Mirandized her and she yelled she didn't need an attorney. She kept shouting that Tommy loved her, he didn't love anyone else. He didn't love Sarah, he didn't love you. He loved only her. If she couldn't have Tommy, no one could…"

"There's your answer," I said. "Just what I said."

There was a slight groan, "Are you going to say I told you so?"

I smiled, although he couldn't see it through the phone. "Probably not if you'll take me out for crème brûlée."

"Why Harper Rogers, I think you're flirting with me!"

I felt like Bambi in the headlights again. This time I think one of the girly girl genes must have sprung loose from wherever it had been hiding...for years. "Um, ah, huh, ah..."

Sam laughed, "Don't worry about it and, yes, I'll take you out for steak and crème brûlée again."

Finally finding my voice, I asked, "Did Lisa admit to hiring a hit man?"

"Yes," he sighed, "she did. She thought if she killed both of them, then she'd never have to worry about Tommy pining for Sarah instead of loving her. Her nephew was killed by accident. The phone number she had for her gun-for-hire is, of course, gone. It was a burner phone. She apparently lost her marbles when she realized her nephew was murdered instead of Tommy."

"She was so calm, though, Sam."

"True, but she was in shock and that could explain her reaction. Also, remember, she wasn't close to her family.

"Anyway, she called him and told him he murdered the wrong man. Since he had seen Tommy in Ronnie's pet store, he figured Ronnie would know where Tommy was or where he was staying. Ronnie, of course, didn't know either."

"How come Sarah's apartment was trashed?"

"She figured if it looked like a robbery, nobody would connect it to the murders."

"Sad, so sad." I could feel tears forming. "I don't think Sarah had any intention of ever hooking back up with Tommy. Maybe that's why she was grumpy or maybe it was because of her new job. Guess I'll never know."

"It's okay, Harper," Sam's voice was soft. "You can't blame yourself. There's no way you could have known any of this."

He paused again. "Lisa's in jail. If she's convicted, which is months away any way you look at it, she's looking at hard time for years."

"All this for someone being jealous. Unbelievable."

"True." Sam paused, and took a deep breath. "Now, about that steak and crème brûlée. When do you want to go?"

Purchase my books at your favorite retailer

Book 1
A Dose of Nice and Murder

Book 2
A Honky Tonk Night and Murder

Book 3
The Faberge Easter Egg and Murder

Book 4
Little Candy Hearts and Murder

Book 5
Lights, Action, Camera and Murder

Book 6
A Turkey Parade and Murder

Book 7
Cookies and Murder

Book 8
Flamingos and Murder

Book 9
Bowling and Murder

Purchase my books at your favorite retailer

| 101 Summer Jobs for Teachers | Kids Fun Activity Book |  Counting Laughs |

About the Author

I grew up in Palatka, Florida, traveled the Southeast extensively for years, and currently reside in Jacksonville, Florida.

To join my VIP Newsletter and to receive a **FREE** book, go to www.SharonEBuck.com/newsletter.

I absolutely love readers because without you I'd be eating peanut butter and crackers. I greatly appreciate you and your support. The best reward I get is when someone tells me my book brightened their day. People are always asking if I'm available for speaking engagements. The short answer is "Yes, of course." I can even do a Zoom event for your readers' group.

Would you be kind enough to review and recommend this book? I appreciate it!

Thank you for being a loyal fan!

Sharon (www.SharonEBuck.com)

Acknowledgements

Thank you to my wonderful support team and friends for your encouragement, words of reassurance, inspiration, and belief in me on those days when the blank computer screen would stare back at me like a one-eyed monster daring me not to write anything. I survived and conquered.

In no special order, thanks to the following individuals:

Kim Steadman – There should be a law about how much we're allowed to laugh on the phone. Thankfully, there's not. Thank you for your friendship and the time we spend talking about writing, books, the book business, and just chatting. Visit KimSteadman.com

Michelle Margiotta – Your music has lifted me up when I was frustrated with my writing process, when I had doubts, and it has nurtured the very depths of my soul. Your music is so filled with colors and swirls dancing throughout your compositions that one cannot help but to be totally enthralled and inspired by your incredible gift. Visit MichelleMargiotta.com

Cindy Marvin – my friend and attorney who tries (hard) to keep me out of trouble before I even get into it.

McDonald's Baymeadows @ I-95, Jacksonville, FL - Keisha and her morning crew for serving me vanilla iced coffee every morning. They jumpstart my day with their smiling faces. It's how I start my day.

Southside Chick-fil-A in Jacksonville, FL – Patty, the awesome marketing manager, and her team have hooked me on frosted coffee. I am now an addict LOL Every fast-food restaurant in America should take lessons in customer service from them. It's always a delight to go into a happy place of business. I am always treated like a friend, not a customer.

George at Athenian Owl Restaurant – Yes, there really is a George and Mama! My favorite Greek restaurant in Jacksonville and they make me feel at home every time I eat there.

And, lastly, thank you to all my loyal readers and fans. I love and appreciate you!

To God be the glory.

Printed in Dunstable, United Kingdom